Murder, She Tweets
(An Eliza Gordon Mystery)

by

Amy Beth Arkawy

For information, email Cozy Cat Press, cozycatpress@aol.com or visit our website at: www.cozycatpress.com

COZY CAT
P R E S S

ISBN: 978-1-939816-81-8
Printed in the United States of America

Cover design by Paula Ellenberger
www.paulaellenberger.com

10 9 8 7 6 5 4 3 2 1

For Mom

PROLOGUE
Los Angeles, CA

"You stole him. Then you killed him. Then you killed yourself. Guess they call that karma, slut!"

"Ma'am, please!" One of the two burly convention rent-a-cops encircling Orchid said. He oozed onion bagel breath and his elfin face was dotted with sweat and acne. She just wanted him to leave. In fact, Orchid wanted the entire SitCom Con crowd to simply vanish. They were just a pack of misfits and freaks (there was a distinct difference between the two groups, and if you didn't know it, well, she didn't have time for you). They were all lined up—five deep—to fetch autographs from Florence Henderson and Danny Bonaduce and one of those girls from *The Facts of Life*, all grown up, fat and with crow's feet. *Pathetic.*

Orchid wasn't interested in any of those has-beens living off ancient fame fumes. She was there for one reason: to confront Bailey Barnes. The only trouble was Bailey was slinking around disguised as some chick called Eliza Gordon—only sometimes she called herself Eliza Chase—who supposedly starred in some lame sitcom as a kid. Only she looked just like Bailey, which made sense since she'd wreaked havoc on Everest Falls only five, six, okay, maybe eight years ago, now. But it was *her* all right. The same smug, well-dressed haughty slut who stole Holt's heart away from Clarice. Poor, fragile Clarice. Like three miscarriages, sudden paralysis, an evil twin and that mysterious blood disease wasn't enough heartache for one lifetime.

"I just want to talk to her," Orchid said, pointing to the *Family Dancing* booth. It was Bailey all right, flanked by a hideous array of thirty-something losers, some college kids and a few tweens, too. She guessed that stupid show had gone into syndication. *Whoop-dee-doo.*

"It's best if you leave quietly," Rent-a-cop One said.

"A little late for that," the second cop said, emitting a Muppet-like giggle that belied his chiseled jaw.

"Choose to diffuse, Chet," Number One said, with a reassuring hospital-admittance-desk smile. *So now we're were in the middle of an* After School Special?

"I won't make a scene," Orchid said, trying to escape the cops' sardine-tin grasp. "I just need to speak with *that* woman."

"Looks like that crazy Carnival cruise has sailed," Chet said, choosing not to diffuse, which actually almost endeared him to Orchid.

It was Bailey all right; she was staring right at Orchid with those, cold, husband-stealing murderous green feline eyes. "Bailey Barnes! I knew you faked it! You *are* still alive!" By now another pair of convention rent-a-cops had joined the party. All of them ushered Orchid out of the crowded hall as people went about their so-called celebrity autograph and selfie hunting business.

"I knew it! Now everyone will know. Just you wait!" Orchid could feel her new Victoria Secret panties bunch up. Not the best day to audition a new pair of skimpies. Well, at least she'd give some strip search Bertha her jollies down at the police station later. It didn't matter now. "I'm on to you Bailey Barnes! You'll get yours! Instant karma's gonna get you!"

CHAPTER 1
Goodship, NY

If the jet lag didn't do her in, Eliza Gordon was pretty sure Soup Opera's new breakfast shift, which she'd added during a bout of fool-hearty winter ambition, would do the trick. But just in case that wasn't enough, that killer Twitter feed she'd launched at the urging of her buoyant college assistants Dee Dee Danziger and Sam Bernstein, not to mention the online mail-order soup biz they vowed to have up and running by fall, would have her stumbling over the finish line in the Exhaustion City marathon.

"Got tired of Tinsletown? Glad to see you back in the real world amongst us mere mortals." Joe Meriwether, straddling an oversized red stool, sounded chipper, but there was a tinge of ire in his voice. *Still miffed over the breakfast business,* Eliza guessed.

"Plenty of real world to go around," Eliza sighed, staring at the coffee pot, filled to the brim with Dee Dee's burnt mud. Joe, the proprietor of Joe's Bottomless Cup, had nothing to worry about.

Eliza was scribbling the daily offerings on the Specials' Board. The same hand that now deftly handled Soup Opera's stubby pink and blue chalk sticks had recently been put to more glamorous use: signing autographs for three heady days in Los Angeles at the third annual SitCom Con. It had been a frantic blur, but sort of fun. Now that *Family Dancing,* the sitcom Eliza had starred in as a kid in the late '80's was finally in syndication, she relished attention from an eclectic group of fans. Even that weird pseudo-incident with a crazed *fan* chanting "Bailey Barnes," the name of the character Eliza had played during her brief stint on the now defunct daytime soap *Day to Day* about seven years ago didn't ruin the rush. Encounters with soap fans were always a little dicey; some fans took the shows seriously—really believed you were the character. And Eliza's Bailey was a real bitchy vixen. Fun to play, for sure, but hard to defend to zealous fans. Still, the woman, whom she'd only glimpsed, had been escorted out so quickly, Eliza could hardly consider it anything but a footnote to an otherwise truly exuberant experience. But while she enjoyed basking in the nostalgic hoopla from time to time, every brush with her past life as a professional actress only reinforced the peace and satisfaction she found in her now *not so new* life in Goodship. All to her mother's chagrin. Poor Margot. Every little thing gave her a glimmer of hope that Eliza would move back home to Hollywood and take the former casting director turned fledgling producer up on her offer of any one of a rotating list of tantalizing *comeback* roles. She was dangling a doozy last weekend: "It's a best friend role. Well, more like best friend of the best friend. But we're angling for Megan Mullally and Sandra Bernhard to star. This could be Mensa's answer to *Bridesmaids*."

"Hey, Hollywood!" Midge Sumner burst through Soup Opera's door, the melodic chimes punctuating her very early visit. "So who'd you walk over this time?"

"What's with you? Pulling Morning Drive all of a sudden? I hope Dandy Dave isn't sick."

"That old workhorse never takes a day off. He'll host a remote from his grave." Midge laughed. "Anyway, if I was doing the morning show, I'd be late." She motioned to the lopsided clock hanging precariously next to the *Duck Soup* poster on the wall behind the counter. Closing in on 8:30 may have seemed ungodly to Eliza, but the Morning Drive gig started at 5:00.

"Okay, so you don't go on until 10. So what gives?"

"The truth is: I've gotten addicted to those early bird scramble wraps," Midge offered a sheepish grin in Joe's direction.

"Ah, my cue to leave." Joe slid off his stool.

"Come on, stay. The truth is: the coffee is still pretty—" Midge lowered her voice and bowed her head, "—lousy."

"Oh, thanks," Eliza offered in mock despair.

"You gotta spread hope when you can."

"I guess you do. And it's nothing I haven't copped to every day," Eliza said, grimacing after taking a bitter sip from her mug. "Why do you think I pop in two, three times a day at the Bottomless Cup?"

"Oh, okay, so you sweet talked me." Joe's face beamed, his shiny mocha dome glistening. "Hit me with one of those famous wraps."

"Two House scrambles, Dee Dee. Stat!" Eliza called into the kitchen. "That never gets old."

"Slave driver!" Dee Dee shouted as she abandoned her latest victim, an uncooperative avocado whose chances of surviving long enough to make it into today's special California Cobb Club wraps were fading by every wayward chop. She went about the more pleasant and predictable task of firing up the stove for the scrambles.

"So who'd you walk over this time?"

"Oh, let's see: just Humphrey Bogart. Oh, and Bette Davis and Joan Crawford. Just to be fair."

"Of course." Midge's eyes widened as Dee Dee deposited a plate filled with a scrumptious scramble wrap, oozing eggs, melted cheddar and gouda, multi-colored peppers, onions, mushrooms and spinach on Midge's Judy Garland placemat

"Thank you." She dove in. "*Egg*-stacy!"

"Unfortunately, I have to concur," Joe said with a sly grin. "But next time, I'm importing the coffee. From across the street."

"Best in the world. I'd be honored." Eliza flashed her winning smile. "Happy customers. That's what we like to see. Right, Dee Dee?"

"Oh, joy," Dee Dee said. The twenty-one year old could already feel droplets of sweat crawling across her spiky white-blonde hair.

"Did you post the specials on the Twitter feed?"

"Not yet."

"I knew this was going to happen. It's like getting a puppy for a kid. They beg, they plead and then Mommy has to walk the darn creature in all kinds of weather."

"Hardee har," Dee Dee scoffed. "I'll do it. I always do it. I'm just not sure we'll have enough avocados to make the cut. They're divas to work with. Something *you* should understand." With that, the young woman, who'd started out two years ago as Eliza's reluctant assistant, charged back into the kitchen to conquer her opponents.

"Well, okay. Guess I've been schooled." Eliza leaned against Soup Opera's counter. "Just let me know if I have to scrap the Club," she called into the kitchen. "She's too much," Eliza said as she spun around facing Midge and Joe. "But I never thought she'd last. I mean she was on academic probation from Connecticut College when she started."

"Youth. Gotta grow into themselves," Joe said, patting his belly. "The rest of us have to rely on your scrambles."

Eliza smiled, nodded as two new customers strolled in and grabbed the window table. "Be right back," she said as she ventured over to take their orders.

"Some people get second chances, even thirds. Some don't even get a time at bat," Midge wistfully offered as she took a sip of coffee. "Seriously, next time, bring over a pot from The Bottomless."

"One House Scramble and a spinach omelet with English muffin, Stat!" Eliza called into the kitchen. She spied Dee Dee shaking her head and grunting over a pair of smashed avocadoes. "Please." She quickly headed to the Specials' Board, and wiped off the Club.

"Oh , and I forgot, Peter Falk," she said slipping back behind the counter next to Midge.

"You forgot Peter Falk what?"

"I walked over Peter Falk's star, too. Tom will get a kick out of that."

"Well, he could use a good laugh. We all could."

Eliza could sense a glum aura suddenly descend around her usually upbeat pal. "What's going on? Oh, right. The letters went out. How did Hannah make out?"

"Bard, Bennington, Occidental, UVM, UMASS," Midge rattled off with glee. Then added in a somber tone, "No love letters from Amherst or Wesleyan. Oh, and get this—the wait list at Quimby. Can you believe? Quimby! That was her safety."

"Fancy. Who knew our local college was such a big deal?"

"We can all blame Deborah Attwater." Midge was referring to Quimby's newly famous Dean of Admissions.

"Oh, right. That *60 Minutes* segment." Eliza shook her head.

"Not to mention that book that got her on the damn show."

"Pretty ironic though, right? I mean she writes a bestseller re-evaluating the need for a liberal arts education, and her own school becomes more competitive."

"Yeah, ironic." Midge commandeered her fork around her plate filled with stray onions and peppers. "And you know what a big fan of irony I am."

"Yeah, but still she got into most of her top choices. I mean she wanted to go away to school anyway, right?" Eliza fired up her small laptop behind the counter, getting set to update the pesky Twitter feed.

"She did until Yolo Steinberg and her magic yams took up residence." Another feather in Quimby College's cap was the controversial performance and mixed media artist who'd just been awarded a prestigious MacArthur *genius* Fellowship.

"Heard she's working up a frenzy with root vegetables for her next project," Joe added.

"Can't you just picture it? *Electric Turnips in Surround Sound Nude*?" Midge sighed.

"Still she's got a good list to choose from." Eliza brightened as she realized Dee Dee had, in fact, updated the Twitter feed. *Spicy Crab & Sweet Corn Chowder #KillerCuisine Today @SoupOpera* topped the list.

"True, but her second choice is now Occidental."

"So? That's a good school, right? I mean, President Obama went there before transferring to Columbia."

"Sure, but it's all the way out in California."

"Ah, Mommy and Daddy want her on a tight leash. I remember those days." Joe offered a knowing smile.

"Well, just a little tighter than Los Angeles would be nice."

"I can understand that," Eliza added "But I can always have Margot take her under her wing."

"Oh, that's comforting."

"Victory!" Dee Dee exclaimed from the kitchen.

"She got in," Midge shook her head. "I mean she wasn't exactly on the Dean's List when she transferred."

"Snuck in under the wire," Eliza whispered, with a muted chuckle. She added *California Cobb Club #KillerCuisine @SoupOpera* to the Twitter Feed. Knowing it was easier to delete the tweet than re-configure the chalked scrawl, she held off amending the Specials' Board again. "Remember, she's a junior now. The Attwater mystique just took hold last year."

"So what does Daddy have to say about all this?" Joe asked, eschewing Eliza's coffee pot with a dismissive wave. "He probably wants her to commute to Quimby."

"Are you kidding? He'd love her to move to L.A. Give him an excuse to expand his empire, build another *Mucho Gusto* bistro and explore a new community of starlets," Midge said. "Far away from his nagging wife's grasp." However long she'd loved Gus Delano, however long they'd been married, Midge had carried the burden of her husband's wandering eye, his well-documented philandering history with her. Even if he seemed to be on his best behavior lately.

Joe winced as his kind gaze met Eliza's.

"You know what kills me?" Midge fondled an orphan strip of yellow pepper, weaving it around her nearly empty plate. "I spent all that time helping them launch the college radio station. For free. So much for community service."

"Hey, come on. All's not lost here. She's on the wait list. And anyway, she probably wants to go away to school. You'll have the whole summer to talk her into Bennington or Bard."

"Maybe." Midge shook her head. "And some kids defer freshman admission. The *gap year* is fashionable these days."

"It'll work out," Joe said, touching Midge on the sleeve of her burgundy and black batik blouse. "These things usually do." With that, he slid off his stool. "I best see what damage Perry—*my* Quimby scholar— has done to my business," he said to Eliza in hushed tones as he reconciled his bill at the register.

"Forget it. Let's talk about something else," Midge said, eyeing the big pastry dome, stocked with a tantalizing array of doughnuts and muffins. A mini-crumb coffee cake captured her fancy.

"Like what?" Eliza, who'd come to read her best friend's edible fantasies with the ease of a soap opera day player's script over the last six—almost seven— years, placed the coveted crumb delight in front of Midge.

"Read my mind." Midge brightened, took a bite. "Michelle outdid herself."

"Not Michelle, Dexter." Eliza shook her head. "I'm giving a new gal—actually, it's a pair—a try. They call themselves—get this—the Pixie Pastry Patrol."

"Oy. A tad on the cutesy side," Midge said. "But they know their way around dough. And competition? I like it. But does Michelle know? She can be a little fragile."

"I don't know. And it's not a competition. I'm still using Michelle's goodies. But she does mostly cookies and cupcakes. These gals have a good breakfast assortment." Eliza nibbled on a cinnamon bun. "Anyway, it's just a trial."

"Well, for the record, your honor, my verdict is *dang, yummy!*"

"So noted."

"Speaking of notables." Midge nodded her head towards the window. Tom Santini, Goodship's handsome police chief, whose romance with Eliza was stalled on a slow simmer, even after two years, was crossing the street, on his way to the popular eatery, a stunning woman by his side. "Did you know he's been hosting a visitor?"

"First I've heard of it," Eliza said, as Tom and his guest pushed through Soup Opera's melodic door. On the plane back from L.A., Eliza had vowed to push the relationship to make or break before summer's end. And at this point, she'd convinced herself, she didn't really care which way it went. But inertia wasn't an option.

"Hi, ladies," Tom said with a slightly guilty glint in his alluring azure eyes.

Eliza didn't need an introduction. She recognized the forty-something, high maintenance, flaxen-haired former beauty queen by his side. Like any familiar ghost haunting a house for decades, the memory of Adelaide La Fontaine had haunted Tom Santini, and by extension his relationship with Eliza Gordon.

CHAPTER 2

Eliza knew where she was going; she just didn't know how to get there. Jonas' office was tucked away on the Quimby College campus in someplace called Knowlton West Annex. And while she'd been to Quimby a few times, it was always to see a film or a play at the Performing Arts Center.

So she strolled the bucolic campus, taking in the fragrant spring breeze, keeping pace with the pulsating serenade of competing Hip Hop and Alternative Rock blaring through dorm rooms. Eliza had a wistful moment considering her own college experience. It had been a catch-as-catch-can after thought, really, just taking classes at NYU and the Actor's Studio in between gigs. Still, she was familiar with quaint campuses. The small college in New Hampshire where her stepmother had taught English Lit was also an idyllic sanctuary. Having battled her way out from under her own domineering mother, Eliza figured Midge's daughter Hannah would be better off spreading her wings farther afield. But if she really had her heart set on Quimby, Eliza hoped Jonas could help pull a few strings. Her late husband Eddie's baby brother, Jonas, had put away his international playboy's playbook (at least for now) and taken up residence as a visiting Associate Professor of Sociology at Quimby.

Students, jacked up on post-spring break hormones, all rushed by in a tattooed, neon-dyed hair, back-packed frenzy. Finally, a young kid wearing a Green Day t-shirt and tattered jeans, tripping over his red Converse high tops, tapped Eliza on the shoulder. "You seem lost, ma'am. Can I help?"

The *ma'am* didn't thrill Eliza, who'd just turned thirty-seven last September, but the appraisal was relative and she was desperate. "Yes, thanks. I'm looking for Knowlton West Annex"

"Oh, that's clear across campus and kind of hard to find. You'd be better off in Beckett, the administration building." He cocked his thumb to the building right across the quad. "They can give you better directions than I could."

Then the kid dashed away before Eliza could utter a *thank you*.

An impressive, ivy-covered stone mansion—the Beckett Administration Building—housed myriad deans' offices: Student Activities, Housing, Financial Aid, Academic Advising and Admissions. The first sign Eliza saw was a placard with Admissions Office and a left-turning arrow. So she followed it, assuming she could get directions there and maybe hear rumblings about the *Wait List* and—if she was really lucky—grab a glimpse of Deborah Attwater up close and personal.

Eliza's inquiry for directions to Knowlton West Annex fetched the same *you can't get there from here* response from the flustered young woman behind the Admissions reception desk. "Guess I'd better get you started with a map," the girl said. As she rose from her chair, Eliza realized that the woman was clad head to toe in timeless L.L. Bean catalog clothes—from her sporty tan headband to her green suede moccasins. The cream mock turtleneck dotted with ducks added the preppie-typecasting finishing touch.

"Okay, I mean it! This is the absolute last time anything like this happens here!" A stern woman's urgent exclamation was coming from a door adorned with the words *Director's Office*.

"No promises," said a male voice, probably younger, dusted with hint of glee.

"I'm serious, Geo. It just can't happen. Not here. My integrity. My reputation is on the line."

"Okay. But sometimes things just happen."

"Not here. Not again. Now get back to work."

"Okay." The big door opened and a young man, probably too old to be an undergrad, emerged. His sandy hair was tousled, his light blue oxford shirt half tucked into a pair of rumpled tan chinos.

Just as the receptionist returned with Eliza's map to a shack or trailer in Quimby's answer to Siberia, the big door opened again. A fifty-something woman—whom Eliza recognized from photos and her TV interviews as Deborah Attwater—peered out. Her expensive tweed suit was rumpled, her stylish gold-tinted hair (was it a wig?) was askew. "Oh, for Christ's sake, Geo! You forgot what you came for." She was waving a folder. But it was too late; Geo had already made his hasty escape.

"Sandy, please," Dean Attwater implored the young woman, who by now was busy circling things and drawing enough arrows to fill a complicated mathematical theorem on Eliza's campus map. "Make sure Geo gets this." She handed the folder to the girl. Did we hear back from the dean at Vassar yet?

"No. Not yet."

"That call gets put through immediately. Whenever it comes in. No matter where I am or what I'm doing. Got that? You have my cell, right?"

"Yes, of course, Dean Attwater." Sandy, looking more harried than earlier, gave Eliza a pleading look. "Be right back." She grabbed the folder and scurried down the hall.

Deborah Attwater gave Eliza a quick once over. She smiled and in a well-honed fundraising tone offered,

"We're in crisis mode around here today. Impossibly busy. But she'll be right back." And with that, Deborah Attwater slammed her formidable door.

"No problem," Eliza said with a smile, noting that such a sturdy door should provide better sound-proofing.

Figuring Sandy's infamous map couldn't get her to Jonas' office, not without a GPS and a trained search team, Eliza left Admissions.

No such thing as coincidence? Eliza burst into laughter as she spied Jonas, surrounded by an lively quartet of students—three girls, one guy (who could have predicted?)—around the corner of the long corridor.

"Look who's here!" Jonas said as he almost literally bumped into his sister-in-law. "If you're looking for the Theater Department, you're lost."

"Actually, I was looking for you." Eliza smiled, acknowledging his groupies with nods. "And there's plenty of intriguing drama right here."

CHAPTER 3

"Here's the thing: it's nothing," Tom said. He was exuding that irresistible boyish charm that belied his forty-four years and could captivate women of all ages and myriad criminal culpabilities.

But tonight, Eliza wasn't buying it. "Sounds pretty Zen for Goodship's no-nonsense police chief." Sure, they were ensconced in a cozy corner booth at *Mucho Gusto*, but Tom had a lot to answer for, and Eliza just didn't know if he was up to the task. And they were beyond romantic ambiance making up the difference.

"So that's how you see me? Still?" Tom's face fell.

"Not entirely." Eliza smiled and waved to Gus Delano who was working the crowd with his undeniable Bill Clinton by way of P.T. Barnum charisma.

The place was busy—not New York City weekend busy—but bustling for a Goodship Thursday evening in early April. As Gus approached their table, Eliza noticed his middle-aged paunch bulging through the tight maroon silk shirt and the oversized black and white pin striped jacket he'd adorned to conceal it. For years, Midge had lamented that her husband's outsized appetites must have been captured like Dorian Gray's on some painting of an obese and wretched character. While he was certainly still handsome with his classic features, jet black hair and seductive smile, Gus' lifestyle was, at least, starting to take its toll.

"Ah, the prodigal star returns." Gus laughed, his rich, infectious laugh. If the good looks didn't get you, that laugh would lure you in. He kissed Eliza. On both cheeks. "Thanks for classing up the place on a weeknight."

"Really? You had to go in for two?" Tom sighed.

"No extra charge." Gus rubbed Tom's shoulders.

"Finally. I catch a break tonight."

"Ah, do I detect a little dissension among the ranks?"

"Something you're all too familiar with, right?" Eliza sniped. She couldn't resist.

"What happened, Hollywood? They worked you over in La La Land?"

"Just let it lay, Gus. Okay?" Tom's twinkling azure blue eyes were pleading with his childhood friend.

"You don't have to answer for me." Eliza took a sip of water, then ran her hand through her long silky honey brown hair. "Actually, L.A. was a pleasant surprise. Coming home was something else."

"Looks like you got some work to do, Tommy." Gus slapped Tom on the shoulder again. "I feel your pain, buddy. I've been there. I'll send over something sweet to ease the burden. But the heavy lifting is up to you" And with that, the epicurean showman was off to glad hand another table of—hopefully happier—customers.

"Are you going to nurse this grudge all night?" Tom asked. "Or let me explain?"

"There's no grudge. But if there was, what makes you think I'd nurse it for only one night?" Eliza took a bite of her shrimp scampi. "Delicious. Want a bite?" Eliza offered with a sliver of a smile.

"Sure." Tom brightened as he delicately ran his fork through her shimmering plate of shrimp and linguine. "Want a taste of mine?" Without waiting for an answer, Tom plopped a puffy square of lobster ravioli on Eliza's plate.

"Yeah, okay. Thanks." She indulged in the savory pasta pillow. "Yum… So explain."

"Well, you met Adelaide…"

"The one who got away."

"Well, yeah…. I guess. Once upon a time. A *long, long* time ago."

"So tell me: what's she doing here? *Now*."

"I'm not sure."

"That's the best you got? Really, Chief? After how many days?"

"She showed up Friday."

"How convenient. The day *after* I went to SitCom Con."

"Come on. You don't think I planned this, do you? You can't. I didn't invite her. Haven't even heard from in her in oh, I don't know, at least fifteen years. I didn't even know where she was."

Eliza delved her fork back into her scampi. *Too scrumptious to ignore even under duress.* Midge's appetite must have rubbed off on her. "So what's her story? You've had nearly a week to figure it out."

"What can I tell you? It's a mess. Mostly manufactured by Adelaide. Her usual nonsense." Tom threw up his hands and lowered his head in a hang-dog that did little to cultivate Eliza's sympathy.

"I didn't know she had *usual nonsense*. I know nothing about this mysterious woman that except her name must never be mentioned in your presence."

"That's Midge's nonsense." Tom looked into Eliza's captivating green eyes. "The not mentioning anything business, I mean."

"I gathered. But you've been so closed-mouthed about her. For years." The *for years* was spiked with a bitter lemon taste Tom wasn't sure he could wash away.

"Look, she's an old girlfriend. That's all. There's nothing beyond that."

"Except she's staying at your house."

"In the guest room. With my father snoring down the hall."

"So having a geriatric chaperone makes the arrangement okay?"

"Don't let my dad hear you talk like that." Tom smiled that boyish Santini smile. He almost ensnared Eliza again. *Almost.*

"This is not about your dad. You know I love Bert. Don't sidestep what's going on here." Eliza did love both Santinis. There was something so decent and kind about them. So irresistibly authentic. *Until now*?

"Okay, she showed up with some convoluted story about her latest soon-to-be-ex-husband's sordid political and or gambling hi-jinx down in New Orleans."

"Latest ex?" Eliza rolled her eyes, sipped her wine.

"Yeah. She's been married three times." Tom flashed three fingers. "Or is it four? Not sure if the latest ex is number three or four." He shook his head, suppressed a laugh.

"Jeez. You shouldn't be dating me. You'd obviously be more comfortable with my mother," Eliza said. Margot had been *0* for *4* in the husband department. So far. Any day she could be waltzing through town with number five. And Eliza figured this one would surely be some boy toy arm candy.

"No thanks." Tom shook his head. "I'm right where I want to be."

"So what does Adelaide's latest ex's exploits have to do with you? Why is she here?"

Tom shrugged. "Your guess is as good as mine."

"I doubt that."

"I'll try to alleviate those doubts." Tom smiled. "Once we get home."

"Home? You mean your house, where we'll presumably find Adelaide drinking cocoa and playing Scrabble with your father by the fire?"

"That picture would make a delightful Christmas card," Tom said. "But I was hoping we could get comfy at your place."

****

By the time they got to coffee and the complimentary tiramisu Gus had sent over, *Mucho Gusto* had erupted into impromptu dinner theater.

A stocky, middle-aged man, wielding a loaf of Italian bread a few tables away, commandeered an audience as he bellowed, "You don't take calls? You don't return calls? You're so important because you've been on *Anderson Cooper?*"

"Please, sir, I'm just having a quiet meal," said the stylish woman seated at the table. Eliza recognized Deborah Attwater. She looked more polished than she had yesterday afternoon at Quimby's Admissions Office. In a slinky royal blue silk dress, with nary a strand of hair out of place, Attwater was preening for something more amorous than an afternoon office tryst. Her dining companion was not the tousled young guy who'd sprinted out of her office, but a tweedy middle-aged man with a balding pate.

"My son would be an asset to the college. He swims, took four AP classes, and scored in the first percentile on the Math S.A.T. Oh, and he plays the oboe, for Christ's sake!"

"Please, sir, this isn't really appropriate here," Deborah's companion offered; the dismissive wave of his hand revealed a charcoal tweed sleeve doused in marinara sauce.

"It's okay, Nathaniel," Deborah chastened. "I'm sure he's very talented," she continued in measured tones, trying to avert her eyes from the man's irate gaze.

"So why was he rejected?"

"So much goes into the admissions' process. And the truth is we have so many wonderfully qualified applicants, we simply can't accept them all." The words were well-rehearsed, but not robotic. Eliza smiled; Deborah Attwater was delivering a fine performance imbued with warmth.

"So that's it?" The man, still flinging the bread, was sweating and turning various shades of pink.

"I'm sure your son will find another school, a better fit. And thrive there."

"Sir, please!" A flustered waiter finally appeared to escort the man out of the restaurant.

Then Gus emerged with his outsized charm. "Come on, fella. This isn't the time or place." He was smiling as he nudged the unhinged man toward the door.

"Fine. Forget it. I'm going." The man pushed through Gus's grasp and as he huffed out of the restaurant, offered one final parental pot shot: "Why the hell did we spend thousands of dollars on oboe lessons? Christ, oboe lessons!"

As the man stepped out the door, an agitated woman burst through the restaurant. Like a laser, the woman, fiftyish with long, unruly red hair, headed straight for the active Attwater table. "This is what you call discretion?" Her voice quavered and her head shook with a fervor that resembled a flickering match.

"Oh, Cynthia, for God's sake!" Attwater's flustered date said, rising hastily from his chair.

"Hope you're enjoying this dinner. It's gonna cost you a lot more than you bargained for!"

"Cynthia, please, you're making a scene," the man said. Eliza noticed he had assorted stains on both his tweed jacket and gray flannel slacks.

Deborah Attwater scanned the crowded dining room—assessing the damage, Eliza figured. "Not here," she said, invoking a similar stern tone she'd used the other day in the Quimby office. "This cannot happen here." She hid her head behind a menu.

"No, not here," the red-haired woman, presumably named Cynthia snipped. "Here is obviously reserved for extra-curricular activities." And with that she grabbed a glass, half full of Cabernet and threw its contents at the indiscreet couple. A few droplets hit the man's already stained jacket, but a substantial splash soaked Deborah Attwater's royal blue silk dress in a most inconvenient location. And then, for added emphasis, Cynthia emptied a basket of rolls on the couple's heads.

"I said not here. This is unacceptable," Deborah said with haughty efficiency. In a move that delighted Eliza, the restrained professional, then took a bite from one of the rolls. "Tasty," Deborah said, as she ran a napkin across her soaked chest.

"Cynthia, please!" The tweedy, sloppy man was now waving a napkin.

"Please, Nathaniel? Pleas are for courtrooms." Cynthia spun around, tripping over her pair of ill-advised black and silver stilettos. "Oh, and when we get to court, make sure to bring your checkbook!"

By now, a team of waiters were scurrying about, cleaning up Cynthia's carnage and apologizing.

After escorting the incensed woman out of his restaurant, Gus stopped back to Tom and Eliza's table. "No extra charge for the two-act play." Gus laughed. "And you thought all the drama in town played out in Soup Opera."

CHAPTER 4

Eliza was in no mood for a Friday night stare down at Peabody's. Just the thought of making strained small talk with Tom in between bites of greasy burgers almost made her wretch. If she'd gone, she would've had to turn the already outrageously loud juke box up to full volume, hoping to drown out her own anger and Tom's evasive half truths with '80's hits and an occasional Sinatra song. But no matter how hard they tried, there would be no dancing around that elephant conveniently in the middle of Peabody's peanut shell covered floor. The elephant named Adelaide La Fontaine had certainly gotten under Eliza's skin.

So she demurred, making a lame excuse about working the Saturday breakfast shift. The fact that Tom didn't protest really ticked her off. Was he relieved? Maybe he really wanted to spend the night with Adelaide, mining her motives and all those long lost charms. So now Eliza was at home, revving up for a night of mindless television, her cats Hitchcock and Tallulah her loyal companions.

Thursday night hadn't exactly ended well. While the theatrics at *Mucho Gusto* had painted the evening in a lighter patina, it was short-lived. By the time they'd got home to Eliza's, she'd rebuffed Tom's advances, offering a mere peck on the cheek. Oh, and a parting shot. "Ever heard of Google?" His aw shucks, "What do you mean?" really stirred her ire. "Sleep on it, King of Oblivion. And call me in the morning." Then she slammed the door with manufactured drama worthy of the soaps.

If she could snoop for clues, surely Goodship's trusty police chief could do so, too. Or he could just ask Adelaide. Eliza guessed he had. So why was he reluctant to share his *old, old* girlfriend's escape plans with his new girlfriend? Maybe he was waiting to get it all sorted out. Or better still: get a firm departure date. Eliza had Googled Adelaide and her ex, *Glorious Georgie* La Fontaine, a colorful and corrupt city councilman from New Orleans. What she'd discovered with a few clicks through cyberspace: he was implicated (though still not officially charged) in a few kick-back schemes—one involving a chain of assisted living facilities and another with the former mayor's cable TV company ties. Though estranged, he was still legally married to Adelaide, and his infidelity was both widespread and widely known. Eliza also discovered Georgie was, of late, a popular topic on a bustling Twitter feed called *Political Husbands Behaving Badly*, whose sub-header read: "*Vitter, Spitzer, Sanford, Oh My.* A cringe-worthy sample tweet:

@PHBB Glorious Georgie so bold. He cheats on wife & mistress(es)! #StandByYourMan?

Humiliating, for sure. But was it enough to force Adelaide to flee the flamboyant city famous for a jazzy free-wheeling lifestyle? Surely the Big Easy could absorb another scandal. And Adelaide didn't strike Eliza as a woman who'd just slither into banishment. Unless it was convenient. But why track down Tom now after all these years?

And what if she liked it here in Goodship? Her quaint northbound exile could stretch out into an easy suburban eternity. Then, Eliza guessed, Tom would have to man up and decide.

Or maybe she'd be the one doing the deciding. Maybe she'd finally give up the ghost. *Curious choice of words*, she thought as she hurled a bag of popcorn into the microwave. "Eddie," she whispered. Of course, she still loved her late husband. But he'd been gone over four years now, and while she still felt his presence, the powerful pull of those spiritual snatches had subsided dramatically since she'd moved out of his family homestead—that cavernous mansion they'd fondly called The Gordon Family Museum—and into her cozy, new townhouse in the Briar Ridge Estates. His last vivid *visit* had come on their anniversary last October. She'd been moved in for about six weeks and Eddie came to her, caressing her as real as if he'd been in their bed. She'd had this experience before, engulfed in a transcendent love, a golden warmth, she could never quite put into words. But this time, Eddie seemed to be not saying goodbye, not exactly, but nudging her forward, giving her permission to share a new love. With a new man. And, though she was, at times, loath to admit it, she had her heart set on Tom Santini.

But something had to give. That slow simmer their romance had been cooking on for two plus years wasn't as delicious as it had been early on. If nothing else, her yearning for a family (before it was too late) would propel them to move forward or shut down the charade. Ironically, Adelaide and Tom's feelings for *the one who got away*—might be the catalyst to either get the whole thing cooking on high or shut it down completely.

None of that would be sifted and sorted tonight. Tonight all Eliza had to do was choose between *Shark Tank* and *Dateline*. Billionaires raising hopes or dashing dreams of upstart inventors vs. murder in the heartland. "So what's it gonna be, Hitch?" she cuddled her corpulent black mush of a cat. "That's what I thought. Murder hands down." The body of a young mother, missing for months, was finally found during the Ohio spring thaw in the woods behind a recycling plant. "It's the husband," Eliza sighed. "It's always the husband." Sure, there was an Internet fantasy lover and a creepy guy who stalked her at work, but Eliza was certain it would be the husband. Hitchcock purred and looked pleadingly into Eliza's face, hoping, no doubt. for a second helping of Fancy Feast salmon. "No go," Eliza said. "Oh, damn!" She jimmied herself off the sunken sofa, the new one she'd bought when she moved. It had seemed so comfy at first, but a few weeks in, and she realized it was too squishy. And Tom always felt too low to the ground when he sat down.

She'd burnt the popcorn. Again. She ditched the ruined bag, tinged brown with shame. That awful burnt popcorn bad day at the multiplex smell permeated the whole house, and would likely linger for hours in the static air. So Eliza opened the windows. She shuddered at that first burst of cool air. The weather had been so variable with warmer than usual spring days and chilly nights. Eliza found the weather, like her own volatile mood swings, oddly exhilarating,

She plopped back onto the couch, a healthier, but less satisfying apple in hand. Ah, the Internet fantasy lover was just eliminated as a suspect—his alibi on the day of the young woman's disappearance, coaching his wife through the delivery of their third child—was rock solid. "What'd I tell ya?" Eliza laughed as Tallulah, her sleek calico scampered by. The craggy *Dateline* reporter with the distinct voice promised more twists before the commercial break. Then the phone rang.

"I know it's short notice, but wanna catch a movie tonight?" It was Jonas, sounding uncharacteristically lonely. His latest vixen *du jour* must have fallen for a shinier offer. "It starts at 9:30. But I think we can still make it to the Quimby Arts Center."

"Uh… okay. Sure," she said.

"Great. I'm on my way. I'll pick you up." The Briar Ridge Estates, on Goodship's outskirts, were closer to Caulfield and the Quimby campus than the Gordon Family Museum, where he now lived alone or with a variety of interchangeable playmates.

"Okay. Ready in ten minutes." Now she'd never know the *Dateline* deal. But she *knew*. Besides the stats that always put the spouse in the prime suspect jackpot, she'd watched enough of these true crime shows to spot the generic jailhouse interview room, and the dubious sweater over prison garb cropped shot. The hubby was guilty.

Eliza rushed about, running a quick blush brush over her cheeks and painting her lips with a seductive coat of Champagne Nights. She swung a favorite blue and green print scarf around her neck and grabbed her well-worn jean jacket.

While Jonas' invite had elevated her mood, Eliza realized the number of years she had left to get away with the fast, no-nonsense natural look were dwindling. Her mother was already appalled that Eliza hadn't "kept up her Hollywood regimen." As if she'd ever had one. Margot was always going on about Botox and injectables. "It's only going to be harder when you're ready." Of course, Margot was referring to Eliza's imaginary comeback. The one she had absolutely no interest in pursuing.

CHAPTER 5

"Can you imagine ditching a teaching job to become a maid?" Eliza and Jonas swerved through the back end of the Quimby campus, in his sporty fire engine red Jaguar, heading to his office in the elusive Knowlton West Annex. Eliza wasn't sure what the urgency was about, but he insisted he needed something from his office delivered somewhere before they headed home. And since she was eager to finally lay eyes on the mysterious locale, and considering she was pretty much a captive, she willingly went along for the ride. They were chatting about *Friends With Money*, the film they'd just seen, starring Jennifer Aniston as the poorest pal in a wealthy and neurotic middle-aged clique.

"I don't know. The janitors around here have a pretty cushy gig." Jonas sputtered a botched attempt at "Whistle While You Work."

"Oh, come on. You'd miss your adoring harem of cute co-eds."

"Obviously, you haven't hung around the maintenance building lately." Jonas pulled into a circular drive and parked the car. As she exited Jonas' Jag, Eliza was pleasantly surprised. It was true Knowlton West Annex was so far at the end of campus, she wasn't sure if they were still in Westchester County, but rather than the FEMA trailer she'd envisioned, the building was a charming and very permanent old stone cottage, reminiscent of the caretaker's place on the grounds of the old Gordon Family Museum.

She followed Jonas into his office, one of four or five housed in the cozy two-story structure. The small room was swallowed up by an imposing oak desk and two outsized brown leather arm chairs and that great bookish smell swirling through the academic clutter of books, folders and studious bric-a-brac. Eliza was amazed that Jonas could have amassed so much in merely a semester and a half.

"Hey, don't know if this helps Hannah's situation, but there's a big bombshell about to blow out of Admissions," Jonas said as he rustled through his desk's clutter, desperately searching for a pressing manila folder.

"Really? What?" Eliza was intrigued. And slightly miffed. Why were they making silly small talk when something big was about to go down?

"Yeah, it seems they erroneously accepted about fifty applicants."

"What does that mean?"

"That means they sent—or actually posted—acceptances to fifty, maybe even more—no one's really sure—kids who were supposed to get rejections. It was a glitch on the website."

"Thanks, I know what *erroneously* means," Eliza snipped. "I meant, what exactly does it mean to the school? Do they have to honor the acceptances?"

"Therein lies the big dilemma." Jonas was now puffing. "Where the hell?" He stepped up his rustling, adding a panicked, frenetic pace to the search.

"Can I help?"

"No, thanks. It happened a few years ago at Vassar, Chapel Hill and a few other schools, too. I think those kids were out of luck."

"Wow! That's pretty cold."

"Tragic. First taste of life's disappointments. Really pity the spoiled brats," Jonas said.

"Show a little compassion, Professor."

He sounded like a spoiled rich ass hat. Jonas certainly had had that pedigree, but Eliza knew he'd also suffered enough emotional blows to cultivate the sensitivity he usually displayed, especially to young people. And while she was sure it was a tricky transference—and it hadn't amounted to more than a single passionate kiss and a mélange of intense emotions—Eliza had shared with Jonas something more than an in-law's affection last summer when he'd returned to Goodship and the family homestead. But since she'd moved into the townhouse, their relationship had morphed seamlessly into a healthy friendly brother- sister arrangement.

"Oh, here! Thank God." Jonas let out an audible sigh. He waved a thick manila folder, labeled *Admissions Reviews, Reccos & Applicant Notes.*

"Does that have anything to do with the impending scandal?" Eliza pointed to the coveted parcel.

"No, I just did some transfer interviews and evaluations. But I know Debbie will be under the gun."

Debbie? Eliza's antennae perked up,

"So I want to get this to her as soon as possible." Jonas tucked the sacred folder into his briefcase and ushered Eliza out the office door with a mobilizing nod. "Whatever they decide to do, there'll be backlash. And poor Deb will be put under the microscope."

Poor Deb? Was Jonas romantically involved with Deborah Attwater? *No, come, on,* Eliza thought. *Impossible. Not his type. But maybe. Who knows?*

They were back in the Jag zipping across campus, with Eliza reflexively utilizing the imaginary emergency brake like she always did when she endured Midge's driving antics. *Maybe I'm an old lady back seat driver type, after all,* she thought.

"I need to drop this at Admissions *ASAP.*"

"Tonight? Won't the office be closed? It's almost midnight."

"Maybe. But I can slip it under the door."

"The building's probably locked up."

"Nah, Beckett's always open. They have a security guard at the main desk." Jonas fiddled with the radio, landed on a progressive rock station from Connecticut. "They have a few dorms stashed on the top floor."

"Really? In the administration building?"

"Quimby's a hot ticket now."

"I know. That's all Midge can talk about. Thanks to Deb Attwater." Eliza almost said *Debbie*, but restrained herself.

"Even before that, the new baby boom nearly doubled the applicant pool."

Eliza quashed a wistful wave. Whether she'd find herself a parent caught up in the whole college expectations and disappointments quandary was to be left for another distant day. "But it's Friday night. Can't this wait until Monday?"

"Probably. But I'm not sure when I'll hit campus Monday. And I promised to get them in."

Before she could even mount a meager argument, Jonas was slipping into a spot in front of Beckett. "It'll just take a sec," Jonas said, sliding out of the car.

"Okay, I'll wait here." Eliza snuggled into the low Jaguar seat.

"Nah, come in with me. It can get pretty creepy and lonely around here late at night."

"Oh, okay." Eliza reluctantly exited the car just as a raucous group of students stumbled by singing a vaguely familiar recent hit song in various states of drunken disharmony.

"Doubt I'd get too lonely." Eliza emitted a half-hearted laugh. "But okay."

Eliza followed Jonas up the curvy cobblestone path and into the administration building. "I'll just slip this under the Admissions' door," Jonas said to the dozing guard on duty at the so-called security desk, as they whisked by without signing in or even flashing an ID.

As Jonas and Eliza approached the Admissions Office, they noticed the door was slightly ajar and a light was on. "Don't tell me she's burning the midnight oil tonight? On a Friday, Deb? Come on."

"Talk about dedication," Eliza mused as they walked through the warm, yet regal reception area.

"Hello? Hello?" Jonas inched further into the office suite. "Deb? Is that you? Deb? You here?" He turned the knob on the Director's Office door. "Burning the midnight oil again, Debbie?"

He walked through the door. "Deb? What gives? Debbie? Oh, God! Deb...bie! Oh, God. No!!" Jonas screamed and a chill rushed through Eliza.

As she ventured into the office, Eliza saw Jonas leaning over Deb Attwater, crying. The woman, hours, maybe minutes earlier, a larger-than-life figure, was now slumped over dead in her executive arm chair, a big bloody gash on her head and a blood-smeared Quimby College snow globe cracked and sitting sideways in the middle of a sticky, wet maroon puddle in the middle of her formidable mahogany desk.

"Don't touch that!" Eliza blurted, a beat too late as Jonas grabbed the snow globe. "It might be... I think it's evidence."

"Oh, my God!" Jonas shouted, as he let the globe drop from his shaking hands onto the luxuriously carpeted floor. "She's dead. For God's sake, she's dead. Someone killed her!"

CHAPTER 6

The phone rang and Tallulah, Eliza's haughty calico, scampered out of the bedroom and down the stairs. After all the hysterical nocturnal commotion last night, Eliza figured the feline had had enough overblown human drama to last at least one of her nine lives.

"Are you there? Oh, God pick up! You have to be there. Please be there. Pick up. PICK UP!!"

"HANG ON!" Eliza shouted into the air as she emerged from the bathroom, still dripping wet in her hastily draped blue terry cloth robe, her hair tucked under a towel. Midge sounded panicked before hanging up with an exasperated thud.

She scuttled down the stairs, discovering Jonas upright, but still catatonic on her couch. "You could have picked up. She's obviously upset, too. Probably heard the news."

No response. So Eliza glared at her brother-in-law; his face unshaven, devoid of expression. Okay, he was traumatized. But so was she, after all. They had both seen Deborah Attwater dead—MURDERED! And it was nothing like she'd ever seen on TV or the movies. Oh, sure she'd enjoyed the puzzle solving of a murder case, but while that was fueled by adrenaline and occasionally fraught with danger it was largely a cerebral enterprise. And certainly nothing had prepared Eliza to stumble upon an actual dead body. She still felt the tumult in her stomach, the waves of nausea catching her in little dizzy eruptions without warning. Before another could cripple her in its grip, Eliza ventured into the kitchen and put on the kettle, setting out mugs and Constant Comment tea bags, hoping the soothing aroma of orange and sweet spice might quell another episode.

"What?" Jonas was now at the kitchen's threshold, still in last night's plaid button down, now untucked, rumpled and drenched in sweat. "What could I say to her?"

"Don't worry about it. I'll call her back." Sympathy wafted over Eliza as she poured the water into two mugs, that delicate mélange of orange and clove caressing her olfactory system. "Have some tea. You'll feel better." She handed Jonas a mug. "Then take a shower." His pungent odor, that desperate smell of rotting onions, propelled another wave of nausea and she fell back into the counter's groove.

Somehow he summoned the energy for the arduous trip up the short staircase and she followed, laying out an old pair of Eddie's boxers, a t-shirt and a pair of sweats that she'd kept for no healthy reason. The exchange might have been awkward under other circumstances, but after last night there were no ceremonies to stand on or explanations to be made.

Back downstairs with her tea and a few quiet moments before she returned Midge's call, Eliza replayed Jonas' manic mutterings. He'd had something of a fling with Deborah Attwater. That all came tumbling out in staccato dribs and drabs during his phone call with his old college roommate Jasper, now conveniently a criminal defense attorney in San Francisco. So he got the sordid tale, such as it was, three hours earlier. Words like "implications," "inappropriate," "tenure," and "termination," flew in nervous riffs from Jonas' lips like a novice jazz singer braving a scat for the first time.

Eliza had called Tom, too, in the wee small hours. Of course, she called Tom, reflexively, only later smarting over the ungodliness of the hour. She'd been too traumatized to make much of the fact that it was Adelaide who answered Tom's cell phone "Oh, good glory lordy, lady!" she'd exclaimed, "Do you have any earthly idea what time it is?" Eliza muttered "emergency," and Tom miraculously got on the line with a brisk bunch of noise about the smoke detector waking up the whole house mere minutes earlier. He said he hadn't yet heard anything, but as Quimby was in Caulfield, the chief there, a guy named Charlie Rosencrantz, whom Tom knew from various county and state police confabs, would be in charge of the investigation. But Tom added, in his most sincere and calming Santini way, that he'd call Charlie "tomorrow… or rather later as we approach a more civilized hour." Then he softened even further and asked how Eliza was doing, offered to come over. With Jonas such a basket case and the sun still an hour or two before rising, Eliza passed on the kindness. She'd heard Adelaide distinctly say, with a bourbon-coated southern twang "Boy, you've got it bad for that sweet chickadee." *Damn straight*, Eliza had thought. And that alone was enough to jolt her out of her state of shock.

"She's dead and I could be a suspect. I think I might be the *prime* suspect!" Midge blurted. Rather than subsiding, Eliza realized her friend's panic may have actually intensified.

"Calm down. What are you talking about?"

"They found her dead in her office. Hit on the head, I think." Midge could barely catch her breath. "Reports are sketchy. But that Attwater bit… *woman* is dead! And it looks like somebody killed her."

"I know." Eliza fell into her sunken sofa, grateful for the cushy landing for a change. "But did you say *you're* a suspect? Why?"

"Not *a* suspect. *The prime* suspect." Midge sounded like her teeth were chattering. Eliza was worried; it was an unusually mild spring morning. Already seventy-five degrees and humid. "Wait! You knew? How?"

"I was there."

"Wait. You were there? I was there!"

"I … we… I was with Jonas last night. We found her… *dead*."

"Oh, God, how horrible." Midge finally took a breath. "But wait, you were with Jonas? What's going on?"

"Nothing. We just went to a movie on campus and he dropped something off at Admissions. That's when we discovered her. Oh, dang. Okay, just wait a sec, okay?" Hitchcock was circling. With all of last night's doings, even the hungry one slept in. Now he was finally sniffing around for food.

"For what?"

"Nothing. Sorry, just my cat. He wants breakfast. Or brunch. It was a late night around here. Everyone's thrown off."

"Oh, great. I'm practically on death row, but the world must come to a halt because your fat black cat is hungry."

Eliza laughed. "First of all, nothing is coming to a halt. I can talk and feed the cat at the same time." Eliza maneuvered herself off the couch with all the grace of an inebriated hippopotamus on roller skates and went into the kitchen, fixing a Science Diet low cal tuna and salmon Blue Plate Special for Hitchcock, hoping he'd leave a few bites for his sleeker calico counterpart. "And secondly, there's no death penalty in New York anymore."

"Very comforting, thanks." Midge was calming down a bit.

"So when were you there? When she was murdered?"

"No! Oh, thank God, no!"

"So why would you be a suspect? What do you mean you were there?"

"I was in her office Friday afternoon. Yesterday. Before… hopefully *way before* she was offed."

"Lovely language." Eliza suppressed a laugh. "Why were you there? That *wait list* business again?"

"Something like that. What does it matter now?"

"Well, it might matter if and when they question you."

"Do you think they will?"

"Well, yeah. If you're the *prime s*uspect."

"What do you mean? Why would I be?"

"I don't know. You just said you were."

"Well, I thought you'd tell me I was overreacting."

"You probably are." Eliza re-filled her mug.

"Did you talk to Tom? Did he interrogate you?"

"No." The very thought of Tom sweating her out in the police station *box* was too ridiculous even for a cheesy crime show. Then that scene with the Quimby security people and a Caulfield patrolman and later that detective propelled her back to the gravity of the whole dreadful business. "The interrogation, as you call it, was pretty short, *routine*, the detective said, just why we were there, what time we found her, that sort of thing. Then he took our names and numbers and off we went." Eliza left out the part when Jonas actually asked if he could leave town and that piercing look the detective had shot back actually sent something resembling a chill up Eliza's spine. Who in real life actually asks that TV cliché question? And why had Jonas been so crazed last night?

"But why wasn't Tom there? Didn't they call him?"

"Nope. Quimby's not in his jurisdiction."

"Oh, right." Midge coughed. "Charlie Rosencrantz is in Caulfield."

"Know him?"

"Yeah, sure. He eats at Gus' all the time. A big appetite for such a slight guy."

"I wonder if Duckheimer will tag along again." Eliza was referring to Detective Fred Duckheimer, an investigator with the Westchester County District Attorney's office whom she and Midge had bumped up against while they sleuthed around two previous local murders. He wasn't exactly a fan of what he called their "amateur antics."

"Oh, God, Duckheimer. I thought you'd make me feel better."

"I'm trying." Tallulah sauntered in. The finicky cat sniffed Hitchcock's paltry leftovers, took a lick of water, and pranced away.

"Well, try harder."

"Okay, for what it's worth, I'm pretty sure there are other suspects. At least two."

"Really? What do you know?"

"The other night, Thursday night at *Mucho Gusto* there was quite a show. Didn't Gus mention anything?" Eliza gave Midge the basics on the middle-aged guy whose son didn't even make Quimby's wait list despite stellar math and oboe playing skills and Cynthia, the spurned wife of Deb Attwater's sloppy date."

"Never said a thing," Midge sighed. "You know Gus never tells me anything juicy."

"What? Talking smack about the husband who schlepped into Caulfield and back with pickles and details, could cost you, lady."

"Speak of the devil, Gus just walked in. I'll switch to speaker phone." Eliza heard a bag rustling and Gus whistling. "But there better be more than pickles in that bag."

"What's going on?" Eliza asked over the loud rustling.

"Ah, ambrosia!" More rustling. "My darling husband was kind enough to fetch me an overstuffed pastrami and corned beef from Max's Last Ditch Deli. Hope you didn't forget the coleslaw. Oh, it's here. Thank you."

"The perfect place to cater your last meal."

"Don't even joke," Midge said with a meaty mouthful of food.

"But you just... never mind, I get it, it's like making fun of your family; it's okay if you do it, but it's off limits for everyone else."

"Nah, my family is fair game. My freedom is another matter."

"Don't worry; I'll bring you an overstuffed every week. With a file in it," Gus jibed.

"Don't start," Midge said.

"Speaking of starting: isn't it a little early for deli? I mean it's just past ten." Eliza had witnessed Midge's hysterical food binges before and was now bracing for the worst.

"So? I've been up half the night. In insomniac hours it's more like three in the afternoon. So I'm already late for lunch."

"What insomnia? You slept like a bear in hibernation. It was after 7:30 when the call came in from the station." Gus laughed.

"How would you know how I slept? You were so busy sawing wood, I'm surprised we didn't get a noise complaint from the Gates of Paradise cemetery across town."

"Well, at least you haven't lost your sense of humor.... or your appetite," Eliza offered. "I'll call Tom back and see what he's heard." Eliza knew Tom hated amateur investigative escapades as much, or even more, than Duckheimer. But this time Eliza figured she could cajole him into aiding her efforts. She wasn't above using his Adelaide guilt to her advantage.

"Good thinking. Oh, for God's sake, Gus you got a round one? You know I like the squares. I gotta go. I'm in the middle of a knish crisis."

"Okay, but wait, before you go, one question: you didn't... I mean you didn't kill her, right?"

"I can't believe you'd actually ask me that," Midge huffed. She took another bite of her sacred deli sandwich. "You're just lucky I'm medicated. Oh, for the record, the answer is no!"

CHAPTER 7

On Monday, Eliza may have had solving Deborah Attwater's murder on her mind, but Soup Opera was embroiled in its own sweet showdown. The brouhaha was in full swing when Eliza arrived at 8 a.m.

"It's fine. I guess after five years, the grass is always greener over the Viking double ovens," a tearful Michelle Dexter was saying to Dee Dee at the counter. "But since no one had the courtesy to inform me..." She plopped her box filled with cookies and brownies on the counter with a fury that shook the plates of four customers enjoying breakfast specials. Poor Andy Orenstein, owner of Aunt Hildegarde's Gifts, was caught mid-forkful and a healthy bite of his spinach and mushroom scramble set sail, dripping eggs on his lovely light green cashmere V-neck sweater before landing on the small radio on the shelf behind the counter. "I still expect payment for this order," Michelle sniffed. "It's only fair." The chubby, middle-aged woman was now in full-blown blubber with tears streaming down her face and onto her purple and red plaid smock top. Her helmet of platinum blonde hair, however, remained intact.

"Okay, but I don't think there should be an issue," a startled Dee Dee offered. "I mean I'm sure Eliza was planning on paying you. She never mentioned anything about not using them. Your desserts are always big sellers."

"What's the matter, Michelle?" Eliza emerged from the kitchen and slipped behind the working end of the counter. "I think there's been some sort of misunderstanding." Eliza had pretty much figured out what was what when she spied Isabelle and another woman, presumably her Pixie Pastry Patrol partner, with an overflowing box of their own huddled at the other end of the counter. "Plenty of room for both. You know we need so much more now that we've added that damn breakfast shift." Eliza bit her tongue. She knew Midge had been right. Michelle *was* sensitive, and Eliza now wondered if she'd subconsciously avoided mentioning the Pastry Patrol gals just to dodge a confrontation.

"Oh, dear. I hope we didn't cause a problem," Isabelle, the tall, rail thin woman with long, limp mousy brown hair, said. She'd been the one Eliza had been working with these past few clandestine weeks.

"I'm sure it'll be fine," Dee Dee said to Isabelle and her partner. Eliza was impressed with Dee Dee; she had matured from the half-hearted, often petulant part-timer into a take-charge and thoughtful manager. In less than two years.

Eliza served up more breakfast talk, emphasizing the need for doughnuts and muffins to Michelle, as her tears trickled out.

"Okay," Michelle said. "But I'm sure I could have handled the extra load. I'm not sure if you know— because I'm never one to toot my own horn, but I actually received an honorable mention in the Hudson Valley Blueberry Muffin Bake-Off six years ago… And you know Phil's still getting back on his feet."

Oh right, thought Eliza, the phony Ponzi scheme scandal that almost ruined her husband's financial planning business, not to mention could have landed him in prison. But that was last summer, and it was just a vicious rumor on a local gossip website. Michelle didn't really have to lay it on so thick. Eliza was a pretty soft touch and she was already nursing pangs of guilt by omission. She should have listened to Midge and fessed up before the two sweet teams ran into each other. *Poor Midge.* Now, it looked like she may have found herself in the middle of another big deal real life drama. Eliza couldn't believe it was less than two years ago when Gus, had, in fact, been briefly considered a suspect in another local murder. *So much for the quiet, small town life.*

"I'm Isabelle, This is Eleanor." The young woman from the Pastry Patrol held out her hand to Michelle, who was now straddling a stool and unconsciously unwrapping one of her own double fudge brownies.

The other young woman, shorter and emaciated, sported a floppy blue hat that reminded Eliza of one Carly Simon had donned on a classic album cover from the '70's. The retro look was cool but it concealed her hair and accentuated her haunting deep coffee brown eyes. Eliza thought the gal looked vaguely familiar, but she couldn't place her anywhere.

"I'm Michelle."

"That's so funny. Imagine that. Belle, El and Shell." Isabelle said, excreting a high-pitched giggle. Dee Dee rolled her eyes as she re-filled coffee cups around the counter.

"Don't get too sugar-coated cutesy," Eleanor said. "Add a couple of our blackberry doughnuts and some people could fall into a diabetic coma."

Even though her dealings had, until now, been exclusively with Isabelle, Eliza figured she was actually more *simpatico* with the other, slightly cynical half of the Pixie Pastry Patrol.

****

After the breakfast shift trickled out and Michelle had departed with something of a wan smile affixed to her face, Dee Dee took her break. She indulged in one of the Pixie Pastry Patrol's famous blackberry doughnuts and whipped out *Hothouse Child*, a book she was reading for her Abnormal Psychology class.

Suddenly, Eleanor, one of the new pastry gals, dashed back into the eatery, frantically searching for a wayward order pad.

"No worries." Eliza grabbed the pad from under the counter where she'd stowed it. "Noticed it about ten minutes after you left. Sorry."

"Thanks. I'm so scattered today. Well if you ask Isabelle... or almost anyone else, I'm scattered every day."

"I totally hear ya," Dee Dee said, looking up from her book. Eliza found that surprising. Her young assistant was busy, always on the move but she never seemed scattered. At least not since her nearly adult transformation.

"They're still using *that?*" Eleanor asked as she spied the book on the counter.

"Yeah, it's a cool book. A little creepy, too," Dee Dee said, flipping through the pages.

"What's it about?" Eliza asked as she wiped down the counter.

"It's a true story about this chick whose parents are both shrinks—so you know they're crazy—watch her like a hawk and impose all sorts of weird rules, and do bizarre experiments on her like forcing her to stay up all night watching horror films. Then they chart her reactions, moods, etc. She must be a certified whack job by now. It was written back in the '90's." Dee Dee shook her head,

"Sounds fascinating. It's a true story?" asked Eliza.

"Apparently," replied Dee Dee.

"I thought it was discredited. Like maybe it was a hoax. Just an easy way for a couple of frauds to make a name for themselves and cash in," Eleanor said.

"Maybe. But if she's out there, she could make a bundle with her own book," Dee Dee said. "Listen to this: 'After the third night of one horror movie after another and limited to only two hours of sleep, Orchid––that's the kid's name, Orchid—eschewed most food except gooey chocolates or popcorn and screamed at the top of her lungs when innocuous children's shows like *The Flintstones* or *Sesame Street* came on television.'"

"What was the point of all of that?" Eliza arched a quizzical brow. "Preparing the kid to live in a multiplex?"

"I told you: total junk," Eleanor said.

"And they do stuff like make her wear shorts without a jacket in the middle of the winter, stumble around wearing a blindfold for days, and force her to sing her conversations with family and in school. So they humiliate her in public and chart her reaction to the reactions of others. And she's only seven."

"Wow. Guess Margot wasn't so bad."

"Cray-cray to the max." Dee Dee waved the book, took another bite of the doughnut.

The chimes startled everyone.

"Too early for lunch, right?" Eliza looked up. "Oh, hi, Lois."

Dee Dee's bird-like mother flew into the eatery in a yellow and turquoise blur just as Eleanor made her second exit.

"I can't believe you're acting like it's just another day," Lois said.

"It's not?"

"Isn't Midge in jail? Didn't they arrest her for that Deborah Attwater murder?"

"What? Not that I know of." Eliza grabbed the counter as she felt her knees buckle. "Where did you hear this?"

"I have my sources." Lois clucked her tongue.

"Well, they're wrong. I'm pretty sure we'd have heard." Eliza wasn't *so* sure, but she hoped Lois was on one of her notorious wrong-way rumor roads.

Dee Dee rolled her eyes. "I'm sitting on a goldmine. I'm living in my own case study." She slammed her book shut. "Guess I'll get started on my own bestseller."

As the girl stalked off with a loud chortle into the kitchen, Eliza called out: "Do me a favor and work the five bean and Manhattan clam first!"

CHAPTER 8

"I wonder what's on the menu at the county jail," Midge mused on the radio as she segued between "Jailhouse Rock" and "Chain Gang."

So at least Midge wasn't behind bars. *Not yet.* So Lois had been wrong. Still, to hear Midge tell it, there was an orange jumpsuit with her name on it down at the Caulfield police station. She'd called Eliza in a frenzy Monday night. "Can you believe they summoned me for questioning?" She'd arranged to go in Tuesday afternoon after her show. "At least they didn't haul me in in handcuffs."

"You'll be fine," Eliza had reassured her. "I'm sure it's just routine."

But Eliza wasn't so sure. So on Tuesday morning around 10:45, after the breakfast business and before the lunch rush, Eliza was driving over to Quimby. *A convenient time to return to the scene of the crime,* she thought. And if something seriously juicy turned up she had confidence that with both Dee Dee and Sam on lunch service, the customers would be in good hands.

Not that everyone thought her field trip was such a grand brainstorm. "Please, Eliza, let the professionals do their job," Tom pleaded over the phone. "Just this once."

"You're a professional."

"Not in *that* jurisdiction." Tom sighed over a cacophony of car horns. "Where are you? In the car?"

"Don't worry. I'm on the hands-free."

"Still." Another heavy sigh.

"Come on; it's not like I drive like Midge." Of course, Eliza now wistfully longed to ride shotgun beside Midge's *Speed Racer* shenanigans. If only she could get her pal out of this potential jam. As she crossed over the Caulfield border, Midge played a peppy WSHP "Locally-rolled oldies" jingle followed by "I Fought The Law." *Oh, God, she's obsessed.* Eliza had visions of Midge locked in the bathroom clutching a bottomless bag of Cadbury Mini-Eggs.

"For the record, Chief, I'm now officially out of *your* jurisdiction. So consider yourself off the hook."

"Where exactly are you going?"

"Guess."

"Oh, for God's sake, Eliza, turn around."

"No can do. Wouldn't want to make an illegal U-turn."

"You know what I mean."

"Yeah, but come on, don't you want to help clear Midge?" Eliza stopped at a light near the entrance of the Shady Lane Motel where she and Midge had helped solve another murder case. "And Jonas," she mumbled.

"Jonas, yeah, what's with you two? You're seeing a lot of him again."

"Not really. Just the one night. Just the one movie and... *the one dead body.*" *God, maybe it's Jonas I should worry about.* Something about the way he'd acted, even before they'd discovered Deborah Attwater's body needled Eliza. That insistence to stop by Admissions when it was past midnight, and the way he'd cajoled her to accompany him when she'd been perfectly fine to wait in the car. And he had touched the snow globe. *Oh, come on! You retired from the soaps, remember?*

"You have some luck," Tom said, "Or I do."

"That's another story entirely." Eliza sighed. Damn, she'd taken a wrong turn and wound up driving through the center of Caulfield. It was similar to Goodship, with tree-lined streets and lovely shops, but somehow not quite as quaint—a thought that filled her with an unexpected sense of pride. *Finally, I really belong. I have a home.* She passed Peabody's Pub on one side and Max's Last Ditch Deli on the other. "Don't you want to exonerate your friends? You've known them a lot longer than I have."

"If she… they're not guilty, they'll be fine."

"What do you mean *if*? You can't really believe either of them is capable of murder."

"Probably not." Tom laughed.

"Oh, you'd make a great character witness."

"I'm just kidding, and a little jaded, I guess. But you never know about people. Under the right—or wrong—set of circumstances, who knows? Anyone might be capable of murder."

"Anyone okay, but not your old friends."

"Statistically that makes no sense. Most murderers are or were at one time somebody's old friends. So if old friends never committed murder there wouldn't be anywhere for you to poke your very adorable nose where it doesn't belong."

"I like the sweet talk, Tommy. I miss it." Eliza regretted uttering the endearment as it slipped from her lips. *There was no time for that now*, she thought, crushing a bittersweet nexus of emotions: yearning, anger, ambivalence, love.

"Me too," Tom said in a sad whisper.

They'd have to leave the romantic reparations, if there were to be any, for later. *Focus,* Eliza thought, as she got her bearings and was now back on Route 1, heading towards Quimby.

"But if she hasn't killed Gus yet I doubt she'd bludgeon Deb Attwater over Hannah being wait-listed.

I mean she doesn't even want her to go to Quimby. We're not talking Harvard here."

"Okay, you make a good case… for Midge. So let's just let it play out."

"You mean like the Adelaide situation?"

"What?"

"Have you figured out what she's doing here?"

"Not exactly." Tom sighed again.

"Sounds pretty evasive." Eliza offered her own sigh, this one an exaggerated artifice. Then she sang along to Midge's latest offering "Suspicious Minds."

"What? What's that?"

"Oh, just singing along with the radio," Eliza said. "Any idea when she'll be leaving?"

"Uh… no."

Eliza sang along with the chorus.

"Okay, I'll meet you at Quimby," Tom said just as Eliza turned onto the college campus.

"I'm here."

"I'm on my way. Please don't get into any trouble until I get there."

"I'll see what I can do. But no promises." Eliza laughed. "Oh, and Chief, don't go over the speed limit."

CHAPTER 9

Quimby wasn't the three-news-van-media circus Eliza had imagined. Not that she knew *what* to expect. But since Deborah Attwater had been so high-profile of late and considering the gruesome way she'd died, she figured there'd be more than a local News 12 van taking up permanent residence in front of Beckett Hall. The driver, presumably the cameraman, but maybe the reporter, was gesticulating wildly as he engaged in an animated negotiation with a Quimby traffic officer. There was also a white sedan with "News 4, New York" emblazoned in black on both sides circling the road in front of the building searching for an open spot.

Otherwise, it seemed like business as usual. Students and faculty were dashing to classes, conferences and lunch. A pack of kids from the track team (or was it cross country?) sprinted by, two by two, in skimpy uniforms. And a trio of hippies stumbled along with trays of melons: cantaloupes, honey dew and watermelon adorned with stickers and action figures. *An assignment for Yolo Steinberg?* wondered Eliza. Everything circling back to Midge and that darn *wait list.*

Of course, the murder by now was four days old and by the standards of the 24/7 news cycle, a stale story. And it would remain so until they at least named a suspect, or, better yet, arrested one. As Eliza ventured through the Beckett Hall doors, she hoped that suspect wouldn't be someone she knew and loved.

The other odd thing: with the exception of a thin strip of yellow crime scene tape, already a mangled mess dangling off the main Admissions Office door, things appeared to be buzzing along as usual in the bustling office suite. Everything seemed normal. Well, almost. Sandy, the harried young receptionist, had been replaced (Eliza assumed temporarily) by a plump Caulfield police officer whose dour expression confuted his cherubic face. Admissions reps—officers, they were called, Eliza guessed—were all milling about; some even interviewing prospective students. *What a selling point*, Eliza thought. *Hey, Mom, hey Dad! Can't wait to visit that school where the Admissions head honcho was just offed!* She spied Geo, one of Deb's conquests, dash by with a handful of folders. In full-tilt business mode, he now sported a dapper grey suit replete with a well-tucked white button-down and a blue and yellow power tie—the image all but ruined as his previously wayward sandy hair was now slicked back with so much gel he looked like a corporate cubicle jockey playing lounge singer during a karaoke luncheon.

Deb's office was another matter. Here the crime scene tape was still firmly affixed to the "Director's" door. *Strange*, Eliza thought. *How can the police get in and out? Surely, they don't re-attach the tape each time?*

"Are you being helped?" Geo asked. "Can I help you?"

"Uh… I'm not sure. I thought Chief Rosencrantz might be here." Of course, Eliza wasn't sure *what* she'd say if and when she went back through that door and came face to face with not only the crime scene she and Jonas had discovered, but also the man who might be trying to put one of her best friends behind bars.

"Do you know if Rosencrantz is still here?" Geo asked the reception cop with a hint of disdain.

"Still in there, I think." The cop waved his hand and Geo stood in front of the office, ran his fingers across the Director's Office placard. Eliza saw an eerie smirk creep across his face. *Was he happy Deborah Attwater was dead? Did he want her job?*

"I don't have time to do your job, guy," Geo said and skulked away. And *if so, ju*st *how badly did he want Deb's job?*

The cop got off his duff and knocked on the door. "Chief, you still here? Someone's here to see you."

"Yes, Jim, what is it?" A tall lanky figure emerged from another door. *Ah, so that's it*. The office had a second door, a hidden entrance that sort of wrapped around the entire suite. Chief Charlie Rosencrantz wasn't what Eliza had expected either. When Midge had described him as "a slight guy," she'd envisioned a short little man. But he was built like Jimmy Stewart in his heyday, tall and cavernous. He was, Eliza guessed, mid to late 50's with a face enlivened by kind blue eyes. Considering Tom's captivating azure eyes, Eliza wondered if such a physical attribute was a prerequisite for all suburban police chiefs. Maybe she could collect photos; if she amassed enough, Eliza figured, she could write—though assemble would be a better word—a bestseller like that book of cake wrecks. Rosencrantz's sparse grey hair naturally fell across his balding pate (not, thankfully, arranged in a ghastly comb-over that so many follicley-challenged men had stooped to). While Tom favored his Goodship police chief uniform, Charlie Rosencrantz eschewed such formalities, donning instead a blue and white pin-stripe shirt, sleeves rolled up to the elbows, and blue slacks, no tie, no jacket.

"Thanks for coming." Charlie Rosencrantz reached out and offered Eliza a firm, but friendly handshake.

"But they told you to come here? The station house would have been fine."

"No problem. It seemed to make sense," Eliza said, making as much use as she could of her rusty improv skills. *So they want to question me, too.* It made sense, of course, as she was one of the two people who'd discovered Deb's dead body. *Just routine.* The words she'd used to comfort Midge really did make sense. And so, too, did it seem routine to question Midge and everyone who'd been seen with Deborah Attwater shortly before her most untimely and unpleasant demise.

Chief Rosencrantz had Eliza recount how she and Jonas had discovered Deb's body. Just the basics: time, circumstance—why they'd come to the office so late, position of the body, the blood. The whole exchange probably took under ten minutes, but to Eliza it felt like hours. Those little dizzy eruptions of nausea gripped her again as she described the blood, actually envisioned the whole surreal scene, almost inhaling that sticky iron smell of Deb Attwater's blood, her last breath of liquid life lingering in the very office where she'd commandeered the college's future. *Ironic,* Eliza thought, *where there had once been strategic prestige, there would now surely be tabloid infamy.*

"So, when did Mr. Gordon—" Chief Rosencrantz paused, poked his pencil at his small notepad. "How are you related?"

"He's... uh, Jonas is my late husband's brother."

"Ah, yes, right." He jotted down a few notes in his notebook. Eliza smiled when she glimpsed the cover: a classic Dick Tracy comic image. Rosencrantz was a lot looser than Tom. Duckheimer, too.

"So when did Jonas pick up the snow globe?"

"Uh, just as I was walking in, I think."

"Do you know why he picked it up?"

"Not exactly. Just an instinct, I guess. I think he was upset. I mean it was... it *is* very upsetting. Obviously."

"Yes, of course." He was a kind man, Eliza could tell. And he'd been at his job long enough to know how to softly interrogate witnesses, to gently extract the information he needed. Eliza wondered if he was as gentle with suspects. She figured he was. Not that she ever wanted to put the assumption to firsthand experience.

"But you said the globe was on the blotter in the middle of the desk and Ms. Attwater was slumped in her chair several feet away."

"Yeah?" Eliza didn't know what to add to mitigate Jonas' action, one she'd found odd at the time. *Loose lips sink ships.*

"Well, it seems an odd instinct to pick it up when its proximity to the body was, shall we say, inconvenient."

"I guess."

"Do you think you would have picked it up?

"I don't know."

Rosencrantz shuffled through his notes for a few seconds that felt like dizzying hours to Eliza who grabbed the edge of the desk to brace for the oncoming emotional tsunami. "Ah, didn't you say you told Jonas, 'Don't touch that. It might be evidence.'?"

"Maybe. Maybe I said something like that. I guess I said that... if it's in your notes."

"That's why it's crucial when feasible to interview witnesses on the scene or as soon as possible."

"I can see that," Eliza said, offering a pensive nod. *Time to shut up now.*

Reprieve came in the form of a small commotion.

"Okey dokey artichokey. Let's haul in the perps and lock 'em in the pokey." Eliza heard the distinctive raspy voice before she saw the short sixtyish woman from whom it had emanated. The woman had broken the crime scene tape and plunged into the Director's office.

"Uh... ma'am..." reception cop Jim said as he staggered behind her. "Sorry , Chief." Then after a sigh and a shrug from Rosencrantz, he retreated back to his reception perch.

"Oh, Sweet Lorraine!" an exasperated Charlie Rosencrantz exclaimed.

"I see Guildenstern is still going it alone in the afterlife."

"You know the tape is there for a reason."

The woman nodded. "To keep out the amateur riffraff. But as a card-carrying member in reasonably good standing of the professional riffraff, I know full well that you've already dusted, photographed and inventoried everything you need. The rest is just show."

"Eliza Gordon, Detective Lorraine Dresser, she's a crack investigator on loan from the Westchester District Attorney's office." Eliza wondered if she was Rosencrantz's personal Duckheimer. The two had obviously known and worked with each other before. And Dresser? Like Duckheimer, whose quacking rubber-soled shoes had personified his name, Sweet Lorraine lived up to hers. She was clad in a flowing brown and green patchwork skirt and a garish multi-colored print caftan-type blouse. Her head appeared to be topped by some sort of auburn shrubbery bifurcated by an audacious print scarf that matched neither the skirt nor the blouse.

"I know you! Watch you on television. Almost every night," Lorraine said in an joyous blurt. "The upside of insomnia."

"Oh, sorry. About the insomnia. Not being seen." Eliza repressed a nervous blip of a laugh. "But I'm surprised you recognized me. I mean I was just a kid in that show." Now that *Family Dancing* was in syndication, various cable channels were running it three, four times a day. Eliza was happy for the recent residual checks, but she didn't want to burn out the franchise.

"You haven't changed that much. It's the same sweet face." Lorraine inspected Eliza's visage in a way that should have been uncomfortable, but somehow wasn't. "Beauty smoothed out the impish edges. How's that for a detective's observant eye?" Sweet Lorraine let out a raspy laugh that sounded like a cough disguised as a bark.

"Lorraine's an aficionado of so many things." Charlie Rosencrantz said.

Lorraine offered a weird little wave. "Anyway, there are other shows or movies. Saw one just the other night. You played a dancer or a veterinarian or something. You were being stalked by an ex- boyfriend."

"Uh, yeah…okay. That was on?" Guess Eliza could expect another residual check in her mailbox soon. "Actually, I played a vegetarian yoga studio owner being stalked by my ex-husband who just got out of prison after killing my new boyfriend." It was one of her last roles, and since it was the type of thing that had been coming her way, Eliza had realized she wasn't exactly on the Oscar track, so it was time to move on. Of course, she was falling in love with Eddie by then, too, so the timing for a new life had been perfect.

"Three swings three misses." Rosencrantz said. "Guess you struck out on that one, Lorraine."

"What strikeout? I got the stalking part right, didn't I? That's the crux of the whole Magilla." Again the raspy cough-bark laugh. "So go revise your score card, Chief."

"Okay, my bad as the kids say." Charlie Rosencrantz smiled. "So now you have a glimpse into the way

Detective Dresser's mind works, Ms. Gordon. Scary, huh?"

"Oh, she's not the type that scares easily. I can tell."

"I guess that's true. Usually," Eliza said.

"Well, thanks for coming in," said Charlie Rosencrantz, ushering Eliza out of the second, hidden door. So that was that. She was summarily dismissed without even realizing it. The only thing Eliza realized: it was *Jonas*, not Midge, they seemed to be focusing on.

"Oh, look. Additional reinforcements have arrived." Rosencrantz chuckled, but Eliza detected annoyance as they both saw Tom Santini, sturdy and handsome in his Goodship police chief uniform, standing in the lobby chatting with cherubic reception cop Jim. "So what brings you to *my* crime scene, Chief?"

"Oh, I'm not here on any official capacity," Tom sheepishly offered.

"I see." Rosencrantz softened as he watched Tom lovingly look at Eliza. He was good at his job. "Well, thanks for coming, Ms. Gordon. I'm sure we'll be in touch again." He shook Eliza's hand and chucked Tom on the shoulder.

"Yes, thanks," Eliza said. As a joke she almost asked about leaving town, but decided against it, noting Jonas' sincere stab at that old chestnut and the suspicious thud it had made as it had landed in the hands of a humorless Caulfield detective just days earlier.

"You can check in, but you can't check out?" Lorraine Dresser burst out of the Director's door, as she'd come in earlier, once again, destroying the newly affixed crime scene tape.

"Oh, Sweet Lorraine! I told you to come through the other door."

"So what ya gonna do? Lock me up and throw away the key?"

"If only I could." Charlie shook his head. "If only I could."

"Satisfied?" Tom asked as he and Eliza left the Admissions suite.

"Not in the least," Eliza said as they started down the hall, back towards the Beckett entrance. "What? Why? Oh, hi!" But the familiar woman, out of place, she'd just spied walked briskly by without uttering a word. "Guess she didn't see me."

"Excuse me? Who?" Tom craned his neck this way and that, looking for a missing person or suspect without a description.

"Oh, nothing. I just saw my baker here. And it threw me, that's all. You know when you see someone out of context."

"Michelle Dexter's here?" Tom peered down the long, curving hallway, now crowded with students and staffers. "I didn't see her. Well, maybe she's taking some Continuing Ed classes."

"Not Michelle. That other gal—Ellen, no Eleanor, I think. She's half of the Pixie Pastry Patrol."

"I didn't know you dropped Michelle."

Oh, here we go again. "I didn't drop Michelle. I've just added the Pixie Pastry people"

"You're cheating on your baker?" Tom regretted the words as the burbled out of his usually restrained mouth.

"*Cheating?*" Eliza asked. "These girls make a mean muffin. Delicious doughnuts, too."

"Oh, right. That new breakfast shift," Tom said, nodding. "That's pretty time consuming."

"Don't tell me you're feeling neglected." Eliza could feel pangs of anger mix with whatever anxiety she'd already been feeling about the relationship and her worries over the investigation.

"No, not exactly," Tom hesitated, glanced blankly at a cluttered bulletin board. "I'm just concerned. That's all. I don't want you to work too hard."

"Why? What else do I have to do?"

They walked in silence out of Beckett Hall. Before they went their separate ways—Tom down the hill to his car, Eliza across the way to a lucky spot she'd claimed—Tom put his arms around her. "Please, let's not end on a sour note here," he said. They embraced. And in broad daylight, with kids and professors passing by, Tom Santini, straight arrow police chief, who usually shunned public demonstrations of affection, kissed Eliza Gordon with all the passion of a condemned man on his final visiting day.

"That's more like it, Tommy." Eliza's mood had lifted.

Tom smiled, and, as Eliza turned to head for her car, he added, "Well, I guess there's an upside to all your extra work."

"What's that?"

"You won't have time to poke around." He laughed.

"Don't count on it." Eliza dashed back to her car.

CHAPTER 10

"What do you want from my life, Mom? It's not like I murdered the woman." Dee Dee Danziger was trying to wrap up an aggravating conversation with her mother Lois as she loaded a take-out satchel for the accountants across the street. Two crab and corn chowder specials, one five-bean, a pair of chicken clubs all went in with ease. It was that pesky eggplant Panini she found vexing; the damn sandwich was too juicy and was already leaking through its durable double aluminum and wax paper wrapping. It was almost as grating to Dee Dee as her crazy mother. *Almost.*

Lois, nursing a tuna and cranberry wrap at the counter, was lamenting the value the Quimby College degree her daughter (*God willing*) would be receiving a year from May. "You'll be singing a different tune, Miss Nonchalant Know Nothing when that diploma isn't worth the price of the paper the diplomas were printed on in 1956."

"The year you graduated?" Dee Dee let out a caustic laugh.

Eliza was happily down counter schmoozing with a trio of fellow Goodship merchants: Georgia Rhodes from Knit Wits, Declan Rinaldi, owner of Cheap Seats Video, and Jill Dondi, the local country market proprietor, whose clam chowder and Diet Dr. Pepper had just hit her Bette Davis placemat. She could take in the contentious mother-daughter exchange from a safe distance. Eliza marveled at Dee Dee's millennial multi-tasking. *Bet she's Googling or updating her Facebook status, too.* She'd admonished both Dee Dee and Sam for texting a few times. But as long as it wasn't a regular thing and the customers were cared for, she really couldn't complain. Eliza was all about picking her battles.

"Don't worry, Lois," Georgia said cheerfully, offering the carefree middle-aged gap-toothed grin of a woman who either by design or luck didn't have a college-aged daughter to spar with or fund. She ambled up to the register with Eliza reluctantly following. "They could start a Soup Opera food truck. Could really clean up near campus and across the county."

"Thanks. Just what I need—another person with a billion dollar idea that will keep my ass moving in high gear." Eliza reconciled Georgia's change.

"As long as you're not planning on working at the Inn full-time." Lois clicked her tongue, making the annoying noise of a rusty game show buzzer. Lois, who ran the pristine local hotel, appreciated her tech savvy daughter's website updates, but couldn't imagine the two working side by side every day for the rest of their lives. "Then she'd have to solve *your* murder!" Lois waved her hand in Eliza's direction.

"Really? You think you can take *me,* old lady?" Dee Dee mocked. "Anyway, I'd rather panhandle. Or open a tattoo parlor."

"Tattoo *removal* will be the new big business," said Georgia, still loitering near the register. "People washing away the regrets of youth and drunken sprees."

"I can give the tattoos in the front and remove them in the back."

"You can start with that!" Lois glared at the little crescent moon tattoo on her daughter's wrist. The ironic thing: Dee Dee, who'd gotten the badge last year mainly to annoy her mom, did, in fact, regret the darn thing.

"Get them coming and going," Georgia said. "Ingenious."

"Why exactly are you still here?" Lois tugged on the flap of Georgia's rainbow print poncho. "Seriously, I've got to get back to the Inn, so let me pay already."

"By all means, pay up." Eliza smiled, as Georgia stepped aside and Lois flashed a pair of crisp ten spots.

"Oh, wow!" Dee Dee blurted, eyes glued to her iPhone. "Oh, God!"

Everyone at the counter and the crowded register clan which now also included Declan Rinaldi and Rebecca, the assistant from the accountants' office, who just came in to retrieve the take-out order, perked up. "What now?" Eliza asked.

"What?" Dee Dee looked up from her phone, took in all the faces staring back at her. Eliza noticed her assistant's face was drained of all color. "Uh, oh, nothing. Just looks like CNN or some cable channel is on campus. Probably to report on the murder investigation tonight."

"Wonderful. Just wonderful," Lois groused. "Better get your head out of your arse, Miss Smart Mouth Not A Care In The World. Enough with that phone and the Tweeter twits. You better get busy making yourself indispensable around here."

And with that, Lois dashed out of Soup Opera. Georgia, Declan and Rebecca followed in short order. But it wasn't until nearly a half hour later, after Jill Dondi's departure that Dee Dee revealed what had so spooked her.

"What's going on, Dee Dee? You feel okay?' Eliza was wiping down the counter as Dee Dee loaded the take-out sandwiches into the display cooler for the commuter dinner crowd. "You kinda looked like you saw a ghost back there."

Her immediate response: "Nah, I'm fine." Then a few minutes later: "Do you know someone named Holt... or Bailey?"

"Who?" Eliza's eyebrows lurched up and she felt herself go a little flush. "What are you talking about?"

Dee Dee showed Eliza her phone, displaying the Soup Opera Twitter notification page.

@watchfuleyes @ Soup Opera: #KillerCuisine, huh? Ask Bailey how she snuffed Holt. #MurdererInPlainSight!

CHAPTER 11

Ghosts from Eliza's soap opera past would have to wait. It didn't matter with how much freaky tenacity that creepy tweet clung to her psyche; things were heating up in the Deborah Attwater murder investigation. At least according to the two prime suspects.

Midge, calling Eliza during a radio break Wednesday morning, had proclaimed herself "in the clear." Her police interview, she told Eliza, had gone smoothly. "Just like you said, it was all routine. In and out in less than ten minutes."

"That's great," Eliza said, a tad dubious. Even she had endured something of a grilling, and Eliza wasn't, as far as she knew, a suspect. But Midge seemed convinced. At least she'd ditched the jailbird Top 40 and was back to an eclectic blend of peppy oldies. While on hold, Eliza had been treated to a few from The 5th Dimension, Petula Clark and The Box Tops.

"Just wish..." Midge's voice trailed.

"What?"

"Oh, it's nothing, I guess. I just wish I hadn't touched that... *that thing*."

"What thing?"

"Oh, damn. Gotta go. The news ran short. There's no spot again. Jeez, Alex better get those sales geeks out of the free trade lunches and out there selling again." Then without missing a beat, Midge was back on the air, an ebullient smile propelling her professional radio voice and a seamless segue into the Dave Clark 5's "Glad All Over."

Driving too fast again. Maybe just a little too fast?

Anyway, while Midge was sure she was in the clear, Jonas was spouting a guilty, "If only" mantra as he paced himself into a dizzy frenzy in the middle of Eliza's small living room.

"Well, you didn't kill her, right?" Eliza tried to contain her exasperation.

Jonas winced. "No, not technically."

"It's a big technicality. Believe me."

"Okay, so I didn't hit her with that... *that thing*." He shook his head, covered his eyes with a sweaty palm. Eliza realized just how handsome Jonas still looked; if anything his angst added a sweet vulnerability to his chiseled movie star countenance. "But maybe... just maybe, I could have prevented it."

"How?"

"Deb was a wreck for weeks. And I pretty much pooh-poohed it."

"That business with the erroneous acceptances?"

"Sort of... well, not really..." Jonas finally stopped pacing and fell into Eliza's sunken sofa. "There was more to it. Or at least, she thought there was." He struggled to sit up on the mushy mound.

"Like what?"

"She'd been getting these threatening letters. Someone was threatening to—" Jonas made rabbit ear air quotes, "—expose her."

"About the applications?"

"I don't know for sure. She made some vague comments about her past, but avoided specifics." He talked about angry ex-colleagues, people who had it in for her since Deb had been a rising Admissions hot shot at Stanford decades earlier. 'Jealous kooks,' that's what I told her, dismissing her fears." Jonas sprung off the couch—Eliza marveled at his agility—and ambled into the kitchen. "Just can't sit still."

Jealous kooks. That's what Gwen Dalley had told Eliza the night before when she'd called the former soap diva to mull over the bizarre tweet directed at Bailey Barnes, the character Eliza had played on *Day to Day.* Gwen had been a true soap star, having played Clarice for over ten years. Since the show had gone off the air nearly four years ago, Gwen had retired to the Berkshires, where she now held acting workshops in an old converted barn. "Some of these fans are serious nut jobs. No lives of their own and plenty of time to fester emotions for fictional characters." She told Eliza about websites, chat rooms and blogs that were still going strong years after most shows had all but shut down. Gwen recounted the time when she'd first started on the show and Clarice was pegged as a bad girl, and a crazy woman confronted her in the produce section of the Food Emporium. "Came right up to me and swung a bag of onions in my face, can you believe?" The shiner she got had to be written into the script and a new storyline developed with Clarice emerging as the sympathetic lead and the start of a groundbreaking series of shows about domestic violence that had earned acting and writing Emmys.

"Think of that creepy fan tweet as your reward. Next best thing to a Daytime Emmy."

"Easy for you to say. You've scored two."

"And I have that whacko fan to thank," Clarice had laughed. "Ain't show biz grand?"

The only thing less grand to Eliza than show business was murder. But solving one was another matter entirely. That exercise seduced Eliza's imagination.

"Were you in love with her?" Eliza asked as Jonas returned with two glasses of seltzer. "Thanks." Eliza took the glass, enjoying the subtly fragrant berry bubbles waft through her senses.

"Deb?" Jonas smiled, sat down in the black high back chair. "No, it wasn't like that between us. Not really. I mean she's… uh…was an attractive woman, with—if you don't mind my saying—a smoldering sexuality."

"Not at all. Go on." Eliza's interest was piqued. While she was far from beautiful, Deborah Attwater had clearly been a woman with voracious sexual appetites and, it seemed, myriad men with whom to satiate them.

"She was a deep person, too. All most people saw was the calculated charm, the ambition. But she had a depth to her." Jonas hesitated, stared into his glass. "This would sound strange to most people, but I think you'll understand… We had a sad soul connection."

Eliza nodded. She did understand. Most people didn't know how deep Jonas Gordon's emotions ran either. He had confided his heartbreak over losing the love of his life, a young British actress to the hypnotic, warped world of a cult years ago. That experience was a catalyst for his career studying and infiltrating subversive groups. It also weighed heavily on the heart of the man most people perceived as a frivolous wealthy playboy.

"The thing is she waved me off. Wouldn't show me the letters. I should have pressed her."

"Maybe she didn't want that. You probably gave her exactly what she wanted. You let her vent, to be heard."

"I don't know. She just kept saying 'maybe it's my fate.' Oh, God!" Jonas shook his head, got up, started pacing again. "But who would do that? Who could hit her… *bludgeon* her with that thing? You know how much force you'd have to use?"

Eliza grimaced. The truth was: she did know. She had killed someone that way. Well, her character had. Okay, so it was Eliza playing Bailey Barnes who'd bludgeoned her lover Holt with a bust of his great-grandfather, Clayton Sinclair, founder of Everest Falls Mills. So, okay, it was a pretend murder being committed with a foam bust with the weight of a Nerf Ball. But Eliza had to conjure the rage and the adrenaline to commit such a crime.

"Why did you pick it...uh... the snow globe up?" Eliza asked, refocusing on the all too real murder at hand.

"I don't know exactly. Charlie Rosencrantz and that Sweet Lorraine woman are fixated on my motives, so I guess it wasn't a smart move, huh?"

"I guess not." Eliza shimmied herself off the darn couch, embarrassed by her less than graceful dismount.

"I don't know why. I had to, I guess. I mean it was smeared with her… *with Deb's blood*, for God's sake!" Jonas was shaking. Eliza thought she detected a tear trickling down his face, but his pacing made close scrutiny a tough call. "It's like I could cradle her. I wish I could have saved her."

"Of course," Eliza said, going to him. She pulled Jonas toward her, enveloping him in a hug. He was sobbing now and Eliza was sure of one thing. Jonas did not kill Deborah Attwater.

CHAPTER 12

Adelaide La Fontaine was on the move. Not that she was moving fast enough, or far enough for Eliza. But Bert Santini, Tom's dad, had had enough of his houseguest. So with a quick call and a whirlwind pack-up, Adelaide was ushered out of the Santini place and checked into the Goodship Inn.

"Lois Danziger should have her running back to the Big Easy in record time," Bert boasted as he started his Friday lunch shift behind the Soup Opera counter.

"I don't know," Eliza sighed. "It's pretty cushy over there. She may take up permanent residence."

"Not if Curious Georgie cancels her credit cards."

"Isn't it *Glorious* Georgie La Fontaine?"

"I don't know from *glorious*, but the whole situation sure is curious." Bert ran a rag across the counter space just vacated by a pair of early lunchers.

"Still no details? Adelaide doesn't exactly come off like the silent type." Tag teaming Bert's clean-up efforts, Eliza handed him a pair of fresh placemats: the random hand of fate plucked Carole Lombard and Clark Gable from the box. "What did you talk about all week?"

"Not much. But it was *thirteen* days. And you bet I was counting," Bert groused. "Just *hi* and *bye*, and always with that phony southern charm. She treated the place like a hotel. Well, more like a motel, I guess. I wasn't exactly offering room service and, thankfully, she wasn't brazen enough to demand it."

"Sounds like you're not a fan."

"Never was." Bert pinched his lips. "Speaking of fans." He nodded toward the door.

"Oh, dear God." Eliza shook her head as the Soup Opera chimes signaled the entrance of Pippa De Long.

"Show time!" Bert chuckled. The local theatre impresario was waving a stack of flyers for auditions for her latest Goodship Community Playhouse production.

"Let the games begin!" Pippa said, as she approached the counter, slipping a flyer in front of Eliza as she hoisted her ample star into an oversized stool. "I'd love a cup of the *soup du jour.*"

"Are you sure? It's spicy tortilla. *Very s*picy." Eliza glanced at the flyer. Pippa was plotting a stage version of *The Great Lie,* a wonderful '40's movie starring Bette Davis and Mary Astor as romantic rivals fighting over hunky pilot George Brent.

"Come on. You know it's never too spicy for me. Not when it comes to theater, soup or men." A youthful twinkle lit up Pippa's incredulously seventy-eight-year-old face.

"Okay. Just don't say I didn't warn you." Eliza headed to the kitchen, spied Dee Dee working the pots. "One tortilla special, Dee Dee. Stat."

"Getting old!" Dee Dee called back, no doubt with the obligatory eye roll.

"So? What about it?" Pippa flicked at her vibrant jade scarf, worked her perfectly manicured hands across the flyer that had tantalized Eliza's attention. "You in? Rehearsals start Monday."

"Don't tempt me, please." Eliza had become the local star at the community theater for a few years running. But with the move last fall and the new breakfast business, she just hadn't summoned the time or energy for the last round.

"I'm all about temptation," Pippa said, wide- eyed as Dee Dee deposited a steaming bowl of the spicy tortilla soup on her Joan Crawford placemat.

Eliza laughed as she hastily surrounded the mat with a few packages of soup crackers and a tall glass of ice water. That spice would hit her soon and Eliza didn't want Pippa to conspicuously have to beg for relief.

"Delicious!" Pippa proclaimed as her cheeks flushed red. "Simply delicious." She worked the crackers as discretely as possible, and Eliza's gaze conveniently scanned down the counter. "My *Doll's House* was such an anemic affair without you. They should have sold iron IVs at the concession stand during intermission." Pippa had regained her composure, Eliza noticed, but the tall glass had been drained of all water and two cellophane packs where the crackers had resided were crumpled in a heap. "Wendy tried; God knows her heart's in the right place. But the girl just doesn't have *it*." As Pippa shook her head, a stray strand of hair slipped from her tight luminous silver chignon.

"Hush, Hush, Sweet Pippa," Bert said as Andy Orenstein slipped by the counter. His wife Wendy had theatrical aspirations that far exceeded her talents. But until Eliza hit town, Wendy's enthusiasm, flexibility and an uncanny knack for selling tickets to a wide network of relatives and friends had almost always guaranteed her the lead. In recent seasons, poor Wendy had been relegated to supporting parts. Eliza understood the lovely woman's pain.

"So you'll do it, right?" Pippa lowered her voice to a perky whisper.

"I'll think about it," Eliza said, mustering a meager smile as Adelaide strolled in. A regal flaxen-haired aging beauty queen, Adelaide still possessed pageant poise and exuded an undeniable confidence. Yet she abandoned pleasantries and slid into a back booth,

patiently waiting for service. *Too good for the counter?*
Okay, let her simmer in her own entitled socialite juices
for a few minutes.

"You want me to handle it?" Bert smiled. "I've
become accustomed to waiting on her."

"Nah, I've got this," Eliza waved him off. Then back
to Pippa: "But *if* I do it, I'll want the Mary Astor part."
That was the juicier role, really, the seductive hard-
hearted concert pianist who steals George Brent away
from Bette Davis' good-natured country heiress.

"Oh, that would be divine. Simply divine," Pippa
cooed. "Wendy could handle a journeywoman's
Maggie. Make everyone forget Bette Davis ever went
near the part."

"Pippa, please." Eliza moved her hand up and down
miming a volume control. "I said *if* I do it. And it's a
big *if*." Since she'd been forced to re-connect with
Bailey Barnes, Eliza figured she may as well play in the
same shrewish terrain. *If she decided to do it.*

"I don't believe in *if*s. Though I've been known to
indulge in a few *and*s and *but*s every now and then."

By the time Eliza got to Adelaide's booth, the
entitled goddess was engrossed in what sounded like a
high-stakes cell phone conversation.

"How many times do we have to go round and
round? You know my terms," Adelaide sniped. She put
up a hand to stave Eliza off. "Sign the papers and you'll
get your precious book back. Sign then retrieve. In that
order. Easy as pie, sugar....Wiggle room? You want
wiggle room? I think you've wiggled your way through
many a lady's room. It's go time, Georgie. No more
time on the clock."

Adelaide clicked off the call, tossed her cell into her
classic monogrammed Louis Vuitton tote. She finally
smiled up at Eliza. There was no getting around it:
Adelaide was a gorgeous woman, always had been,

always would be, and she was all too aware of the power all that natural beauty could wield. "I'll tell ya, darlin,' some men are incorrigible... and I've had my share."

"I'm sure you have," Eliza offered, without cracking a smile. "So what can I get you?"

"I don't know," Adelaide blankly stared at the menu. "Maybe I should go for an old standby. Can you make a grilled cheese?"

"Sure, we can do that. Maybe start with the *soup du jour*? It's a nice *mild* tortilla."

"Okay, sure." Adelaide handed Eliza the menu. "Sometimes there's nothing like an old reliable favorite. If you know what I mean, darlin.'" No matter how thick she laid on the southern charm, Eliza knew exactly what she meant.

"Be right back," Eliza said as she walked back to the kitchen.

"Take your time. I'm not going anywhere."

And I'm not about to hand Tom Santini back to you on a silver platter.

"Okay," Eliza said, tapping Pippa on her jade scarf-draped shoulder. "I'm in; Let's put on a show!"

CHAPTER 13

Paranoia collided with perverse humor on Saturday night at the Quimby College gallery. Eliza flinched, then sort of half-laughed as she gazed at Dee Dee's canvas. Photographs of Twitter feeds with the words TWEET and DELETE superimposed stared back at her. The piece's inherent irony, it's (hopefully) unintentional mockery followed Eliza as she and Tom moved about the gallery, taking in an array of student art—myriad abstract blotches, mixed media collages, washed out landscapes.

Dee Dee? Oh, no, God no. Eliza swatted that fleeting accusation away like a pesky fly. It was the girl, after all, who'd tried to shield Eliza. Late Friday afternoon, with only a smattering of last ditch lunchers loitering about Soup Opera, Dee Dee and Sam were at the counter huddled over an iPhone. "I keep telling you: you can't delete other people's tweets. Only block them," Sam had said with exasperation.

"Oh, right. Okay." But before Dee Dee could do any blocking, Eliza, brushing by with the pre-wrapped take-out sandwiches, spied that second unnerving tweet.

@SinisterSuds @SoupOpera Bailey Barnes SLAUGHTERED Holt! What will she do 2 ur lunch?! #DeadlyDining

"Just a crank," Eliza had said, hoping her acting skills were honed enough to mask her shock. "Nothing to worry about." She had offered a dismissive wave as she scurried back into the kitchen.

"No candidates for the Met," Tom said as they stopped in front of another splotchy canvas. "Won't even make the cut at MOMA."

"Don't be so sure." Eliza smiled, forcing herself back to the present tense. She recounted her sojourn through the famed modern art museum some years back when she'd witnessed an energetic group of school kids running through one of the galleries. One boy, maybe nine, ten tops, almost knocked into a slab of linoleum, cordoned off with a rope and a plaque that read "Bronx Floors." His friend tapped him on the shoulder and uttered: "Don't touch that. It's art.... I think."

Tom laughed and Eliza did, too. She hadn't told Tom about the creepy tweets. Why worry him about something that was probably nothing? Nothing he could do about it anyway. And besides, there was a real crime to solve. The very real murder of Deborah Attwater. Of course, Deb may have had some warning. Jonas telling Eliza about Deb's threatening letters ran through her mind. *Not the same thing. Nothing to worry about. Not now, anyway.*

Eliza waved and nodded as she saw Dee Dee and an unfamiliar young guy with wayward neon green hair walk through the crowd. "You haven't seen my mother, have you?" Dee Dee seemed anxious. "Rumor has it she's planning on showing up."

"Well, of course. It's opening night. I'm sure she's proud of you," Eliza said. "But no, I haven't seen her yet. Hi, I'm Eliza Gordon." She reached out her hand for Dee Dee's friend.

"Oh, sorry; this is Dylan." The boy, who had haunting coal black eyes, grunted *hello* and shook Eliza's hand with all the assurance of a sweaty bag of

Wonder Bread; then shoved his clammy paws back into his tight black and red pinstriped slacks.

"Jackson Pollock didn't have great manners either." Dee Dee chucked Dylan on the shoulder. "He did that sculpture by the door. Got him an MFA fellowship to NYU."

"Very impressive. Congratulations," Eliza said, recalling the big oddly-shaped abstract sculpture that greeted patrons at the entrance.

"And congrats on your piece, too," Tom said. Eliza thought it was a nice gesture even though she was pretty sure he didn't know which one was Dee Dee's.

"Very provocative," Eliza added, regretting the comment even before it landed.

"Oh, thanks," Dee Dee said. Eliza was relieved that the girl was too pre-occupied with Lois's imminent arrival to say anything about her prescient subject matter.

Dee Dee and the taciturn Dylan guy moved on, with Dee Dee still scanning the crowd for her mom. "A portrait of the young artist with Lois Danziger as her mother," Tom quipped with a sympathetic nod. For a moment, Eliza could picture Tom Santini as a doting dad at school plays and little league games.

"I hate to remember what I looked like at that age with Margot as my mother."

Tom put his arm around Eliza's shoulder. "Poor baby... but you were already famous by then."

"You mean I was already a has-been by then."

"Think it's more complimentary the way I said it."

"More comforting too." Eliza let her head fall into Tom's arm fold.

They were in front of a beautiful-ugly photographic display of homeless people when Dee Dee sprinted back over. "I'm guessing you spied your mom," Eliza offered.

"No, she's still M.I.A.," Dee Dee said, breathless. "I just realized... oh, God, you saw it, right?"

"It's okay." Eliza tried to meet Dee Dee's gaze with an imploring look.

"I did it a long time ago. Way before... Oh, God, I'm so sorry."

"It's fine, really. Don't worry about it."

"Are you sure?"

"Of course." Eliza gently grabbed Dee Dee's hand. "It's really an intriguing piece. You should be proud."

"It's just... I feel bad because... oh, great, she's here." And with that, the girl dashed back towards the entrance.

"What was that about?" Tom asked.

"Lois has her unhinged."

"But why was she apologizing to you? Something about her piece bother you?"

"No, of course not. It's cool. You heard me tell her."

"Okay, but she seemed..."

"Take the night off, Chief, will ya?"

"Hey, stop stealing my lines, lady."

"Oh, wonderful." Eliza spied Dee Dee with her mother and Lois' plus one.

"What?" Tom looked over, too. "Oh." His face fell and suddenly he became entranced with his shoes and the shiny gallery floor.

"Goodship's Oprah and Gayle," Eliza muttered as Lois and Adelaide sauntered over.

"Y'all taking in what passes as culture in this town?" Adelaide asked.

"Bored with us already?" Eliza took in Adelaide in all her designer grandeur. It didn't matter if she was overdressed in a sparkling sleeveless number. She was captivating. If she stayed in town, Adelaide La Fontaine would easily become the local trend setter and fashion icon.

"Bless your heart," she said, petting Eliza's marginally fashionable violet gauze tunic with deliberate condescension. *She actually had the temerity to whip out the classic Southern put-down?*

"I'm just getting started, darlin' There are lots of intriguing people here. As *you* well know, things could get downright *spicy.*"

CHAPTER 14

@QuimbyConfidential: Cops swimming in right pool, but need to change lanes! #KillerProf

Talk about bad timing. Jonas was on the lam, but the Quimby Confidential Twitter page was pointing to new suspects.

"It's not wise, that's all I'm saying," Tom said, and he was saying it with coleslaw dripping from his mouth in between bites of his overstuffed brisket sandwich.

"What can I tell you? So my life's basically one big food crawl," Eliza said as she negotiated the Triple Threat, a behemoth corned beef, pastrami and salami combo. "I gotta size up the competition." They were hunched over a utilitarian aluminum table at Max's Last Ditch Deli Sunday afternoon. So far she'd sized up the food as delicious and the décor as something else. The walls plastered with old license plates and vintage Wild West and 1930's gangster WANTED posters were cool kitsch but the tables seemed like rickety diner leftovers and the chairs practically ejected you with their lack of comfort.

"Well, it's a good thing you have a good metabolism." Tom smiled, looked into Eliza's entrancing green eyes.

"Amen to that," Eliza said. She smiled, and for the first time in a long time, let herself truly enjoy a light moment with Tom.

"But I was talking about Jonas' disappearing act."

Eliza shook her head. "There's no disappearing act. He just went away for a few days to clear his head." She didn't mention how far he'd gone: San Francisco, presumably to visit his old roomie Jasper, the criminal defense attorney. Maybe they'd strategize and Jasper could hook Jonas up with a local legal eagle. *And maybe*, Eliza thought, *Jonas would also travel to Palo Alto to dig into Deb Attwater's past at Stanford.* Not that he'd confided anything like that, but Eliza could see his sleuth wheels turning. *Takes one to know one.*

"Well the timing isn't great," Tom said, now playfully stroking Eliza's luscious honey hair. "Especially with all the talk." There was a mischievous, even slightly titillating, look in Tom's eyes that Eliza found very seductive.

"So let people talk. It's not like you can shut them up anyway."

"That's for sure." Tom smiled as he watched traffic flood in and out of the busy Last Ditch Deli door. "But it's just not smart. Not now. Not at this point in the investigation."

"And what point is that exactly?"

"Couldn't tell you—" Tom began.

Eliza joined him in his familiar refrain, "Not my jurisdiction."

"You need a few new lines, Tommy." Eliza coyly waved a French fry—a long thin, perfectly crisp specimen—in Tom's direction.

Tom laughed. Eliza loved the way the crows' feet made his enticing azure eyes dance. "How's the show going?" Tom changed the subject with the seamless grace of a man accustomed to controlling the conversation.

"We don't start rehearsals until tomorrow night."

Tom nodded. "Oh, right. Well, it should keep you pretty busy."

"Not *that* busy." Eliza snickered. She knew what he was thinking, and he knew she knew. And they both knew she'd be sleuthing, even if she had to do it in her sleep.

"You're so beautiful." He gazed into her eyes.

"Keep sweet-talking me, Tommy. It's working."

"Speaking of sweet," Tom said as he and Eliza both spotted Midge and her daughter Hannah trudge through the door. Right behind them was a striking woman: tall, thin, sixty-something with spiky rainbow punk hair. Midge cajoled Hannah into snagging a place in line right behind the woman and then the insatiable DJ sprinted over to Tom and Eliza's table. "Right there! I'll be right there!" Midge waved to Hannah, who still wore a disgruntled teenage scowl like a badge she was reluctant to retire.

"Slumming?" Midge took a deep breath as she took in the spicy aroma of deli meats and pickles.

"Cheating on me again?" Eliza offered a mock sigh.

"Cheating? Look who's talking." Midge cocked her thumb at Eliza. "Michelle Dexter gave me an earful."

"She's still upset about that?" Eliza said. "I don't have time for the drama."

"Really?" Both Midge and Tom looked askance.

"Really." Eliza buffered a laugh.

"You see that woman in front of Hannah?" Midge asked in her version of a whisper which suspiciously sounded like a normal speaking volume for most people. "Yolo Steinberg. Larger than life."

"Ah." Eliza nodded, offered Midge a French fry. "Think Hannah will talk her up for a leg up on the *wait list*?

Midge shrugged. "Hope not."

"Guess they'll have to drop down to the list for sure this year what with the scandal," Tom said, now shielding the fries from Midge's zealous hands.

"Don't bet on it." Midge shook her head. "Kids today? The notoriety alone will probably garner even more applications." Her quick fingers managed to snag another fry. "But I overheard Hannah last night talking up Bard to her friend Tinsley."

"Well, there you go." Eliza smiled.

"So what's with the Attwater investigation? Are they closing in on a *real* suspect yet?" Midge grimaced, still squirming from her brief stint in the hot seat.

"Not in *his* jurisdiction," Eliza said, coquettishly tilting her head in Tom's direction.

Tom winced, threw up his hands. "Can't you watch the news like everyone else?"

"Oh, here's breaking news: Vegetarians at the gate!" Midge said as she eyed the line and saw Yolo Steinberg place her order: tabouli salad and rice pudding. "Thin as a rail, punk rock New Age vegetarian. Who could have guessed?" Midge scoffed. "Better get in line before Hannah screws up the knishes." And with that, Midge dashed to her daughter's side.

"Oh, this should be good," Eliza nudged Tom.

"Midge's knishes?"

"Nah, remember them?" Eliza nodded as a couple brushed by their table. It was Deb Attwater's sloppy date, Nathaniel, and his unhinged estranged wife, Cynthia, from that volatile night at *Mucho Gusto*.

"Oh yeah. Very observant."

"Good detective material, right?"

"I'm not encouraging it." Tom shook his head and offered Eliza a bite of his brisket sandwich.

"Don't do anything to disrupt the apple cart. Not now, Cynthia," Nathaniel said as he snagged a table near Tom and Eliza's.

"Okay, okay, I said I'd go along with the gag. For now. But time's running out."

"Enough, Cynthia." Nathaniel took off his washed-out blue windbreaker and slipped it around his chair. Eliza noticed it was stained with blotches of sticky yellow, brown and red. "You won't be happy if all the money goes to lawyers."

"Oh, you'll be up to your busy boxers in lawyers. *Criminal* lawyers. People are already talking."

"That's what I mean." He spied Yolo and made a beeline for her table.

"Incorrigible," Cynthia snarled and she darted to a shelf filled with fancy and expensive snacks.

Incorrigible, indeed, Eliza thought. "Any word on Adelaide's departure?"

"What?" Tom flinched.

"When is *the one who got away* going way?"

Tom shrugged. "She's not staying with us anymore."

"I know. But from what I hear it was Bert's handiwork that got her tossed."

"Come on; let's not ruin a great day," Tom pleaded, and the sweet look in his eyes made Eliza retreat. Besides there was too much other immediate drama to enjoy.

Now Eleanor, the less familiar half of the Pixie Pastry Patrol, had just strolled in. "Hi," Eliza said, as the young woman skulked by, offering only a weak wave. Eliza saw her trounce over to Yolo Steinberg's table.

"I was waiting. Where were you?" Eleanor hissed as she stood in front of Nathaniel.

"Not now, please," Nathaniel said. Then to Yolo: "Sorry."

"This can't wait. I got another letter from the dean." Eleanor tried to lure Nathaniel away from the table with a tug on his stained faded denim shirt sleeve.

He shook his head. "Cynthia is here. It's not exactly convenient."

Eleanor snorted. "My situation isn't exactly convenient either. I guess there are no second extensions in the Quimby graduate program life."

"Maybe if this was only the *second* extension—" Nathaniel offered a wan smile.

"Don't forget: you owe me!" Eleanor blurted as she stalked back towards the door. "And I always collect!"

"A moveable feast and a traveling show," Midge mused as she and Hannah, bags of deli take-out in hand, stopped back at Eliza and Tom's table. "Watch out for new developments. I'll call you later for an update." Midge swiped a few more fries for the road.

"Don't worry. She'll take notes," Tom said.

Before long, Cynthia returned to her table with a bag of expensive honey-dusted cashews and an even more precious jar of imported olives. Finding only Nathaniel's jacket, she scanned the place. Eliza could almost feel the heat of Cynthia's fury as the woman discovered her husband was still loitering at Yolo Steinberg's table and now rubbing the artist's shoulders.

She stormed the table, something, Eliza noted, seemed to be one of the woman's highly cultivated talents. "I thought you were in line," Nathaniel tried to sound casual.

"Unbelievable!" Cynthia snipped.

"What's your problem now?" Nathaniel was still cozy with Yolo, who by now was working on her rice pudding, a placid smile affixed to her doe-like face.

"Not *my* problem, Nathaniel," Cynthia fumed. "It's *your* problem. That cart you keep talking about, it just toppled over."

"A work of living art," Yolo offered as she rose from her seat and headed for the restroom.

"There's nothing here to get so worked up over." Nathaniel shook his head. "Go get yourself a sandwich.

And get me a salami on rye, maybe some extra pickles to take home, too."

"You're a real piece of work, but hold the art," Cynthia huffed. And then just as Chief Charlie Rosencrantz and Detective Lorraine Dresser walked into the busy deli, she added, "How convenient. You can turn yourself in and get your last free meal to go."

CHAPTER 15

There was no getting around it: Eliza was being held hostage by Twitter. The entire weekend she'd spent looking at, thinking about or forcing herself *not* to think about checking the @Soup Opera Twitter notification page. Only two venal tweets. *So far.* But she knew there'd be a third. Then a fourth, fifth, six, God only knew how many more. She just didn't know *when* the next one would appear. The ironic thing: Eliza rarely even kept her phone on; she'd always scoffed at the people whose devices were attached like extra limbs. Always thought they were branding themselves Big Brother's parolees, signing up for voluntary ankle monitoring. But now a crazed *fan* had made her a cyber prisoner, condemned to an indefinite sentence.

"What's with you?" Midge snapped her fingers in Eliza's face. "Fallen in love with your phone all of a sudden?" It was Monday afternoon, after three, and Midge was lingering over a bowl of the soup *du jour*, red pepper and gouda. So Eliza confessed her obsession with the creepy tweets.

"That's the price of fame," Midge quipped.

"I'm not famous." Eliza sighed. "Never was."

"Famous enough for *Dancing with the Stars* or *Celebrity Apprentice.*" The women had often mused how many of the so-called stars on those shows were celebrities with a lower case *c* written in invisible ink. "Wait, you're not really worried about this, are you? It's just some crank, right?"

"Yeah, probably." Eliza mustered a smile as she wiped down the counter for the umpteenth time in the last ten minutes even though Midge had been the only one sitting there for the last half hour.

"So what does the Chief have to say?"

Eliza's shoulders slumped. "I haven't exactly mentioned it to him."

"Ah, so what's what with you two?"

"Nothing." And that was exactly the problem. For as much levity as they'd enjoyed the last few days, there was still nothing of a forward motion in Tom and Eliza's relationship. And Eliza feared if a certain someone didn't leave town, any scintilla of hope to get their romantic train back on a speedy track would be long gone. "Just antsy to see the one who got away go away already. Did you ever meet her? I mean back then?" Eliza half-laughed, knowing she sounded bitter, maybe even a tad desperate.

Midge shook her head. "Never laid eyes on her before she hit town two weeks ago." She retrieved a cracker from a cellophane packet. "He was down in Vanderbilt, I was up in Vermont when the heartbreak went down. Don't think he talked about it to anyone. Not Gus or even Eddie. One day they were engaged, the next day it was off. "

"And no one asked anything? I mean that seems pretty uncharacteristic for you guys."

"Not for self-involved college kids out making new friends, new lives. Anyway, when he came home that Christmas, he looked so... so devastated and, honestly, I guess we all just thought it was better to follow his lead."

Given Tom's taciturn nature when it came to personal business this meant he shut them out and let the humiliation and, hopefully, the heartache fade.

"Well, at least she's out of the Santini house," Midge offered. "It's a step in the right direction."

"Yeah, but she's gotten awfully chummy with Lois. Can you believe she actually showed up with her to the student art show at Quimby Saturday?"

"Why not? It's not like the bird has had a date in over a decade." Midge eyed the pastry dome. "Any day-olds you wanna unload?"

Eliza smiled, fetched a gooey rum raisin doughnut she figured wouldn't fare well overnight. "Try this," she said, placing the confection on Midge's Mae West placemat.

"What was he like? Lois' ex?"

Midge shrugged, setting her eyes on her doughy prize. "Sort of a vague person. Walked around foggy and laconic." Midge enjoyed an enthusiastic bite from the pastry. "Wow, so good!"

"Right? Michelle will just have to deal." With so much positive feedback and sales to fuel it, Eliza just didn't have time for Michelle's nonsense. Those Pixie Pastry Patrol gals were keepers. Even if she kept running into Eleanor, the one she knew the least, in strange places, with the girl behaving oddly.

"I'll second that emotion!" Midge blurted. Then in a more subdued tone: "But I'll tell you, once those divorce papers were signed, Dwight David Danziger shot out of Goodship like a bat out of hell. He hightailed it faster than if I'd driven him myself."

Eliza laughed. "Dwight David? As in...?"

"Yep, he was named after President Eisenhower. His parents were big Republican Party mucky-mucks. I actually think Lois married him for his name.... thought it gave him some sort of prestige, instilled in him some grand ambition. But he was happy working that same back room banking job Lois' father had arranged when they got home from the honeymoon."

"Parents can really screw up kids just with a name sometimes." Eliza bit her tongue.

"Don't start." Midge had years ago confided her own name was a tribute to her mother's devotion to the miniature Tootsie Rolls—Midgies. "It's been a burden but I think I've done my sweet name proud."

"It suits you," Eliza said with a smile.

"I just wished I never touched it… that thing… that snow globe," Midge said in one of her weirder segues. But since her friend's voice was awash in a sudden anguish, Eliza didn't point out the *non sequitur*.

"But why? You said you were in the clear, right?"

"For the murder, yeah. But my fingerprints have to be on it."

"So? How would they even identify them? Unless you've been bonded. Or wait, you didn't rob a bank, did you? Or a candy store?"

"Hilarious!" Midge lightened, offered a mock eye roll. "No, it's just… I don't know. I touched it… the murder weapon. Just thinking about it, creeps me out, you know?"

"Yeah, I guess." Eliza could see that. On the other hand, she had Jonas who *had* to touch the snow globe for the very reason that repelled Midge. Both, she figured made sense.

*****

The freaky soap "fan" tweets still held Eliza captive on Monday night during the first rehearsal of *The Great Lie* at the Goodship Community Playhouse—which was basically a table read—forcing herself to twice grab glances at the Twitter page. The first one was early on when Colin O'Neal, who was playing Pete, the pilot of both leading ladies' affections, had a sneezing fit. Seventeen sneezes, one juicy enough to entice Pippa De Long to surrender her blue and red print scarf for the cause, before Eliza lost count. The page was filled with the usual suspects: people serving up pithy praise for the soup and sandwiches *du jour*; a few waving red flag warnings over the spicy tortilla soup (Eliza was perfectly happy pretending they all came from Adelaide); and a slew from Jill Dondi, who since her grandson had activated her Twitter account two weeks earlier, had become an incessant tweeter. But no "love" notes from @WatchfulEyes, @SinisterSuds or any other untraceable disposable Twitter handles.

Eliza's second surreptitious glance—which blessedly also came up empty—happened during the last scene, when a ringtone to the tune of "Baby Love" jolted Wendy Orenstein out of her chair and into the middle of what her frantic husband Andy described as a "major twin toddler meltdown." One, it seems, that had involved a box of rare and very expensive vintage wind-up clown toys that had erroneously been shipped to the house instead of Aunt Hildegarde's Gifts. "What can I do about it?" Wendy sighed as she sheepishly slipped back into her seat. "And why would I wanna rush home now?"

But the interruption was enough for Pippa to call it a wrap. The clock was closing in on 10:00 anyway, and Eliza suspected Pippa was a furtive *Real Housewives* fan who yearned to get home to see what overblown scandal was reaching a fever pitch in Atlanta, New Jersey, Beverly Hills or whatever franchise of the inexplicably popular reality TV trash fest was featured that night. "Very nice," Pippa cooed, clapping her hands. "Now memorize your lines. Crawl into the very soul of your characters' lives."

"Oh, I just told Andy I'd be another half hour at least," Wendy said as folks went about gathering up coats and bags. "Guess I just bought myself a reprieve I don't know what to do with." She exhaled a weary mother laugh.

"Too bad they roll up the sidewalks around here before nine. Or we could have all gone dancing," Colin said as he slung his black laptop satchel across his chest. Then he darted out of the theater, presumably to go home to his own wife and kids.

"I'm so glad you wanted to play Sandra," Wendy said to Eliza. "I wouldn't know how to *crawl* into that that... you know... playing someone, a person who could do that. A woman who could give up her own baby." Wendy hoisted a big, weathered canvas tote, brimming with diapers and toys, over her shoulder. "Oh, sorry."

"For what?" Eliza stole another glance at the Soup Opera Twitter page. Nothing new. *Phew.* She surrendered the phone to her bag, vowing not to check again. At least not until she got home.

"You... well, it's just... well, you don't have kids."

"So?"

"Oh, nothing. Just...well, maybe you can't understand that maternal pull... maybe you don't even want to have kids."

Eliza shook her head. "Well, those are two separate things." Eliza knew what Wendy was getting at, and, frankly, she found it insulting. People with kids seemed to think only other parents had been imbued with a special brand of empathy. But if birthing children guaranteed some miraculous transformation, why were there so many negligent, violent or just plain bad parents running around screwing up generation after generation of kids? Eliza's bemused assessment of her own mother's maternal pull landed Margot somewhere between the brazen stage smothering of Mama Rose in *Gypsy* and the cold petty conditional love of Betty Draper Francis on *Mad Men*. At least Margot's maternal instincts hadn't been fueled by the unstable meanness of Joan Crawford in *Mommie Dearest*. But any inherent sweetness she possessed, any loving inclinations Eliza displayed, she'd always credited to the few weeks she spent every summer during her formative childhood with her father Ernest Chase in New Hampshire. And when she was a teen, he remarried a nice woman, a professor named Pamela, who never had any fulltime children of her own, yet offered nothing but loving kindness to Eliza.

"I do think I can understand. As an actor you have to be able to feel what your character feels, even if you've never experienced it. Otherwise, the performance won't be authentic. And you may as well send the audience home to read a book."

"You're right." Wendy looked so diminished, Eliza felt bubbles of guilt seep into the snobbish gloat she'd been basking in. "That's why you're the pro and I'm just a hapless amateur."

"You're not so hapless," Eliza softened. "And I *used to be* a professional. Now we're all in the same boat."

"Not quite." Wendy smiled. "But thanks for saying it anyway."

"Oh, and as far as the other goes—I do."

"Do what?"

"Want kids," Eliza said. Aloud. For the first time to anyone other than Eddie.

CHAPTER 16

By Wednesday, with nary a new nasty tweet and breaks—or rather leaks about imminent breaks in the Deborah Attwater murder investigation—Eliza backburnered her anxiety and re-focused her attention on the case. And she was picking up deliciously official tidbits during the bustling lunch shift.

"She's my oldest friend. How was I supposed to know she'd spill the beans?" Sweet Lorraine Dresser hung her head as Eliza delivered cups of cream of asparagus and black bean chorizo to the back booth the detective was sharing with Chief Charlie Rosencrantz. The two had obviously sought refuge in Soup Opera, away from the white hot glare of the Caulfield and Quimby College spotlights.

"Why were you feeding her beans she could spill?" Rosencrantz asked as soon as he thought Eliza was out of earshot.

"What can I say? She plied me with lemon daiquiris and, let's just say, my tolerance isn't what it used to be." Lorraine offered a little girl caught with her hand in the cookie jar smile. "If it makes you feel any better I'm still recovering from that Tilt-A-Whirl ride my queen-sized waterbed turned into."

"It doesn't. And thanks for the visual." Charlie shook his head. "She's in the media, for God's sake, Lorraine."

"Media schmedia. The woman's got a blog and a podcast," Lorraine sneered. "It's like talking over a fence. Oh, this soup is delicious." She took a big slurp of her cream of asparagus.

"Never underestimate a yenta with a fence." Charlie sighed. "Anyway it's out now and we'll just have to deal with it."

"What's to deal with? Just keep stonewalling."

Charlie shook his head, spun his spoon around his soup "I've already dodged calls from News 12 and *The Journal News*. Oh, and the *Quimby Confidential*—those kids could be the most dogged."

"Student newspaper? Good luck with that." Lorraine let out a low volume version of her bark-cough-rasp laugh.

"They don't bother with that anymore. It's all done on Twitter."

"Keep up, Pops."

"I'm sure I'll have to keep up with inquiries from all the major New York City and cable outlets soon. How much you wanna bet there'll be a stack of new media messages when I get back to headquarters?"

"How 'bout a week of lunch here?" Lorraine beamed as Eliza returned with their sandwiches: the Sloppy Joe special for her, grilled salmon club for Charlie. "The rumors were right. The soup is to die for."

"Thanks," Eliza said, smiling. "Hope the sandwiches live up to the hype, too."

"I'm sure they will," Charlie said with a nodding smile Eliza recognized as her cue to exit the scene. She obliged, though she moseyed back to the kitchen in slow-mo.

"Delicious!" Lorraine exclaimed, sharing a juicy Sloppy Joe bite with her garish print tunic.

"Jeez, Lorraine, you're almost as messy as..." Charlie noticed Eliza was taking the long way home, chatting blithely with the customers at the next booth. In hushed tones, he continued: "You know I like to have all my ducks in a row before making an arrest. But we don't want this guy to get skittish and skip town."

Oh, no, Eliza thought, as Poppy Sumner and Georgia Rhodes blathered on about the annual Spring Carnival next month. *Jonas? Technically he had already skipped town. Tom was right. This doesn't look good.*

"What skip town? I mean where's he gonna go? He's got tenure."

"Oh, Sweet Lorraine. You kill me."

"Not yet. Let's wrap this baby up first. Then I'll do you in and arrest myself." Lorraine threw back her head, the shrub on top waving as she spewed a loud, juicy version of her cough bark laugh.

*****

@QuimbyConfidential Closing in on Big Deb's killer? This could get messy. #SloppyProf.

So they think it's *him*? *Nathanial Miller*? Eliza nodded as she glanced at the Quimby Confidential twitter feed. But why? Eliza was nursing a frothy brew of emotions. Relief loomed large, as she realized maybe, just maybe, Jonas was off the hook. There was also the thrill she felt when embroiled in a case, even if she had nothing to do with solving it. *Not yet anyway.* But there was also that dubious feeling she got when she was perplexed by murky motivations. Yeah, okay, police don't have to have motive to make an arrest; heck, prosecutors don't even need it to score a conviction. But it sure helps to know why the alleged culprit would commit the crime. Especially one so serious, so heinous as murder.

As the lunch crowd dwindled, Eliza punched in Jonas' cell number. She hadn't heard from him since he took off for San Francisco, and that was nearly a week ago.

"Oh, hi. Are you back?"

"No. Soon though," Jonas said, over a crappy connection. "….if I still have one."

"Oh, I'm pretty sure you still have one," Eliza said, piecing together that Jonas was talking about his job. "Think you're off the hook."

"…on to some…"

"What?"

"Think I may have some…. inf… Deb's past."

"At Stanford? Something with those jealous colleagues?"

"What?... no… it's more per… think…"

"Where are you? When are you coming home?"

"Palo..soon….more stop..L…" Crackling now.

"Okay, please call me later."

"What? Okay...closer than…."

"What? Hello? Jonas?" Damn. The signal had faded. She was left in the cellular void.

When Eliza looked up from the phone, her eyes locked with the steel grey eyes of an unfamiliar man.

"You don't make anything in the neighborhood of a crawfish chowder or gumbo, do you?" the man asked with a whiff of a Cajun accent. Handsome, in a rugged middle-aged way, the guy offered a sly smile. "Look at me: I've just hit town and already I'm homesick."

CHAPTER 17

@QuimbyConfidential Hot Mess Profess Makes
Arresting Scene #KillerCampusComotion

Charlie Rosencrantz's ducks had lined up alright,
and morphed into media vultures. On Friday, the
Caulfield Police, accompanied by officers from the
County, hauled Nathaniel Miller, squirming in
handcuffs, out of his senior seminar, aptly called "F.
Scott Fitzgerald and the Dissolution of the American
Dream."

"Did they really have to make such a spectacle out
of it?" Eliza was actually feeling sorry for the sloppy
suspect as she and Tom were riveted to the coverage on
the evening news.

"Standard procedure," Tom said, trying to wrestle
the remote from Eliza's clutches, as he sank ever deeper
into her squishy sofa. "But we don't have to watch it
non-stop. It's not like there's been anything new in the
last few hours."

"It's so awful. Sam said it was pathetic." Eliza's
young assistant Sam Bernstein had been on campus as
the cops had escorted Professor Miller, described on the
TV news as "a fifty-eight-year-old, previously popular
tenured English professor, with seventeen years on the
Quimby College faculty, accused now of the murder of
the school's high-profile admissions director, Deborah
Attwater, fifty-six, with whom he may have had an
adulterous affair." *Previously* popular? Already? And it
was apparently a cringe fest, the way they made that

poor man do a perp walk across campus. Sam had said the place was awash with reporters. On the news they showed a sea of microphones bobbing up and down as the cops escorted him through the quad, screaming, "I didn't do this! I couldn't... wouldn't! I didn't kill her!" The last humiliation (for now) came as the cops were loading Miller into a van and the poor guy hit his head on the door. "A big goose egg on the top of his head," Sam had said, almost breathlessly, "I was that close to him; I could see it. God, it was like a TV show only better... or worse. God, it was so surreal, you know?"

"I don't get you," Tom said. "I mean, I thought you'd be doing cartwheels."

"Why?" Eliza shot him an incredulous look.

"Midge and Jonas are in the clear. Isn't that what you wanted?"

"Well, yeah. Sure, of course," Eliza, still with a firm grip on the remote, flopped back into a more comfy position, now nestling her head into Tom's arm fold. "But this just doesn't make sense. It doesn't feel right."

"Oh, here we go."

"Well, does it? Tell me: don't you think there's something wrong with this arrest?"

"I don't know. It's not...."

"Don't you dare say it, Tommy. It's like nails on a chalkboard already."

"Okay, I won't say it. But it's true. And we don't know what evidence they've got. Charlie Rosencrantz wouldn't make an arrest if he didn't have solid proof. Trust me, I know him well enough to vouch for that."

"But why would Nathaniel Miller kill her? There's got to be a motive, right? I mean his *wife* would make more sense."

"I don't know. They could have had a lover's quarrel. Or maybe she was threatening him, holding something over his head."

"Like what? Okay, so they were having an affair, but it had been on full display at *Mucho Gusto*. Remember? You were there. So what was she holding over his head? I'm telling you, Cynthia makes more sense."

"Maybe if this was a soap opera," Tom sighed, "Then you could re-write the script. But this is real life."

"I'm well aware of that, thank you very much," Eliza snipped, playfully tossing a pillow at Tom.

"Okay, so then you also know in real life things aren't always so neat."

"I know, but they still have to add up. And this just doesn't."

"Give it time." Tom maneuvered his tall, muscular body out of the mushy sofa with a remarkably graceful dismount. "Now it's time for dinner. Wanna do take-out? Maybe Lucky Pearl?" He stretched, then walked into the kitchen; he'd been comfortably ensconced in Eliza's place long enough to know where she kept the menus. "What do you say maybe some Sweet and Sour Shrimp or some Low Mein?" Tom was back in the living room now waving the take-out menu.

"Do you think there's a smoking gun?"

Tom shrugged, shook his head. "Dunno. But there's a hungry boyfriend who could kill for an order of Lucky Pearl Hot and Sour soup and House Low Mein."

"Okay, order it already." Eliza clicked off the TV, jimmied herself off the sofa with the lithe dexterity of an elderly rhino and went into the kitchen to set the table.

*****

"With the assistance of a wise man, you will solve a most perplexing problem," Eliza pretended to read the thin white strip she pulled out of her fortune cookie.

"Come on. What's it really say?" Tom shook his head as he grabbed for the fragile fortune paper.

"Alright, alright," Eliza pulled away. Then for real: "The person who learns to laugh at himself will never cease to be amused."

"That works." Tom laughed.

Eliza grabbed her phone off the counter and stole another glance—her third so far that night—at the @SoupOpera Twitter notification page. She didn't want Tom to know, but she just couldn't resist. If he noticed, he wasn't letting on. For that she was grateful. And for the dearth of new nasty tweets.

"Now yours." She smiled coyly.

"You will kiss a beautiful woman." Tom balled up his little strip and leaned across the table, pulling Eliza in for a kiss.

"Okay, I won't challenge it." Eliza said and they moved from the kitchen into the living room, landing back on the couch. "See I can suspend my suspicions."

"I like the sound of that." They shared a few moments of uninterrupted passion.

When Tom came up for air, Eliza was already working the remote, turning on the TV again.

"Oh, come on. Nothing new, right?"

"Let's see." The anchor seemed to re-hash the earlier report, with footage of the embarrassing arrest. "Still feel bad for the guy."

"Even if he did it?"

"Well, yeah. Not as much, I guess. But still the humiliation. He'll never live that down. No matter what." Eliza couldn't help herself, she was sucked into the cable TV vortex.

"You're too much."

"Look who's talking."

"What do you mean?"

"I mean you're in the wrong profession, Chief."

"How so?"

"For a cop you have a curious lack of curiosity."

"Oh, I'm plenty curious." Tom tried to tempt Eliza into another romantic embrace. She resisted, so he played along. "It's all about priorities, lady."

Eliza gazed at the ceiling. "Don't say it."

"Never crossed my mind." Tom bounced off the sofa; another impressive exit.

"I mean even with Adelaide?"

Tom sighed. "Talk about nails on a chalkboard."

"Okay, but come on, Tom. You didn't even ask why she showed up. Here? After all this time?"

"I asked. Of course, I asked." Tom was pacing around the living room now. "I told you what she told me."

"But that's so vague. Didn't you press for details?"

"No. I figured she told me as much as she wanted to tell me."

"That's it? It would drive me nuts."

"Frankly, I wasn't that interested. And. well, I guess I just didn't want to get swept up in all her drama again."

"She broke your heart big time, didn't she?"

"I guess. I don't know." Tom paced, avoided eye contact with Eliza. "I… we were so young. I think I imagined a lot of it. She liked the looks of me, I guess."

"Well, that I can understand." Eliza smiled.

Tom returned the gesture, but his smile was wistful. "Thanks, but I mean she liked the looks of the package: a clean cut Yankee from a nice family, a good looking town. You know she visited one Thanksgiving and fell in love with the place.

"So far our tastes are on the same page." Eliza wanted to find fault with Adelaide's predilections. So far, no dice.

"But it didn't last. It couldn't, I guess. She met a better looking prospect. A true southern gentleman, Elias Hampton Graham III, with political aspirations, a family very big in bourbon circles and a bottomless trust fund she was dying to dive into."

"So she just called off the engagement?"

"Not exactly. One day she just stopped wearing her ring. That's how she told me it was over."

"And you never asked her about it? You didn't confront her?"

"Of course, I did. But she just acted like it had all been a joke, or a fantasy. I think she said something like: 'We'll always be such special friends. You'll always be my one and only Yankee.'"

"How... I don't know... shallow and weird." Eliza shook her head. "Did she give you the ring back at least?" Eliza hoped Tom had sold it. She certainly didn't want a ring with tainted juju. *If it ever came to that.* \

"Her father arranged for the ring. I couldn't afford the ring she expected—deserved." Tom laughed. "I still can't. God, that thing was so huge. It was embarrassing. When I think about it now... and I hardly ever do... the whole thing was so embarrassing."

"Well, you were so young."

"Exactly. It was more of an infatuation, I guess. I mean, what does a twenty-year-old kid know about real love? Anyway, Adelaide could never really have given me what I needed. She's just not capable of a deep connection, of really loving someone. It's not her fault. That's just the way she's wired."

"To be a heartbreaking shallow bitch?"

"I would have been a little more generous in my phrasing, but yeah, that sums it up."

"Did you know Glorious Georgie is in town?"

"Good. Hopefully, he'll take her home."

"So that's it?" Eliza sighed.

"What do you want me to say?" Tom fell back into the sofa. "I just don't care that much." He crossed his arms.

"Okay, Tommy." Eliza could see the sadness in his eyes.

"What I *do care* about is how insecure her being here makes you feel."

"*Insecure?*" Eliza flinched; even if that's exactly the way Adelaide's presence had made her feel, she didn't want to look pathetic in Tom's eyes.

"Unhappy, then. Irritated. Whatever. I don't like the way it's put a wedge between us, that's all."

"I'll second that."

"I don't love her." Tom took Eliza's face into his strong, gentle hands. He looked pensively into her bewitching green eyes. "I mean, can't you tell? Look at you. Look at me looking at you. I love you."

"I love you, too." Eliza welled up a little and they embraced. "But I think we've got some work to do."

"Let's get started then." Tom pulled Eliza off the sofa. "Upstairs."

CHAPTER 18

"Big surprise. The man's a slob," Miriam Sussman said, a sliver of disdain accenting the turkey and avocado wrap, and bottomless lemonade she'd been nursing at the Soup Opera counter for the last two hours.

"Guess that's what did him in," Georgia Rhodes, said, a copy of the *Goodship Citizen Gazette* draped over her plate, concealing her sloppy half-eaten eggplant Panini. "They say they found Deborah Attwater's blood on his tie. Along with mustard, strawberry jam and tomato vodka cream sauce."

"Disgusting!" The scowl on Miriam Sussman's face made Georgia so self-conscious, the aging hippie hastily brushed off crumbs from her blue and green tie-dyed tunic.

So that was it? Eliza whisked by, refilling coffee around the counter. A blood-stained tie seemed like a flimsy smoking gun. *But how else could Deborah Attwater's blood have landed on Nathaniel Miller's tie?*

"Well, sloth is one of the Seven Deadly Sins." Miriam tapped her empty glass. *And hogging counter space should be number eight.*

"Okay, but I'm cutting you off." Eliza forced a smile as she refilled the retired high school librarian's glass for the fifth or sixth time.

"I abhor arbitrary rules." Miriam grimaced as she leisurely twirled the straw in her glass.

"That's all they've got?" Eliza turned her face to Georgia. "There has to be more evidence than that, don't you think?"

"Well..." Georgia panned down the page. "That's about it."

"And how'd they got their hands on the tie? Did they even have a warrant?" Eliza's suspicious mind was working overtime, envisioning Cynthia planting the evidence like the scorned wife in Scott Turrow's *Presumed Innocent*. She could've planted the tie and then blithely let the police in, practically luring them to the closet and the so-called smoking gun.

"Says here: 'Caulfield Police presented the suspect with a warrant last week at his apartment right off the Quimby College campus, where he's lived for the last few months after separating from his wife of twenty-one years.'"

"Oh." *There goes that theory.* Seems Nathaniel and Cynthia were, in fact, leading separate lives, or at least living in separate residences. So Eliza doubted Cynthia planted the tie. She probably didn't even have access to that apartment.

"Also says: 'Sources say Miller became the prime suspect after a witness relayed what was described as a volatile confrontation with Ms. Attwater late Friday afternoon. The disgraced professor's fingerprints—along with those of dozens of others—were also found on a Quimby College snow globe the Admissions Director kept on her desk as a conversation piece—now believed to be the murder weapon.'"

"So that's that." Miriam smacked her lips as she buttoned up the conversation.

"Maybe. Maybe not." Eliza wasn't letting Miriam have the last word. She still hadn't forgiven the old crank for the misery she'd spread throughout town last summer when she and her nephew spewed hateful accusations and rumors across *The Goodship Grapevine,* a local gossip site they secretly ran. The worst offense had been publishing naked photos of Jill Dondi at Woodstock. That alone was tempting enough for Eliza to ban Miriam from Soup Opera; and she'd do it, too, if she wasn't sure the curmudgeon would hit Eliza with a lawsuit. "What's the motive? Do they mention a motive?"

Georgia carefully scrutinized the article. "Nope. They just end with 'Calls to Miller's counsel were not returned by press time.'"

"They don't need a motive," Miriam sniffed. "For someone so hell bent on inserting yourself into every investigation in the area, you clearly have little handle on the law"

"I know they don't technically *need* a motive. But it sure helps. Especially with a jury."

As Eliza swung back into the kitchen she heard Miriam's parting shot: "That one thinks life's one big soap opera."

Everyone's a critic. But as Eliza worked the (thankfully) rapidly depleting pots of black bean and lobster bisque, she mulled her own motives for clinging to this case. Why did she really care so much? Tom was right: her concerns about Midge and Jonas being suspects seemed to have been eroded. So why did she still feel so invested in the outcome? Well, for one thing, she rationalized; she and Jonas had been the first ones to stumble upon the murder scene. *And Deb's dead body.* And, yeah, okay, she also had to admit she was a natural sleuth. And once she was hooked on a case, there was no letting go. Not until it was solved. And this one just didn't *feel* solved to Eliza.

****

Dee Dee burst through the swinging kitchen door waving her iPhone. "Okay, I know you said it was nothing but..."

"No, don't tell me." And she didn't have to. The gloomy look on Dee Dee's pasty grey face said it all. Another tweet had arrived.

"Yeah, sorry." Dee Dee flashed the phone at Eliza. "But I think you should see it."

@DeadlySudsSpecials @SoupOpera #NathanielMiller & #BaileyBarnes What's it take to wipe #Murder off the #Menu?

"This one's worse, right?" Dee Dee's voice slightly quavered.

"I don't know. Let's not get carried away over some prank."

"I'm not so sure that's all it is. I mean this one's almost a threat."

"I wouldn't go that far." But Eliza knew Dee Dee was right. And she also knew there'd be more.

"Have you told Tom?"

"No."

"I think you'd better."

CHAPTER 19

A mediocre cloud hung over another lackluster rehearsal at the Goodship Community Playhouse Monday night. And Eliza couldn't pin the blame on her amateur co-stars. She was the one dropping lines faster than that most recent menacing tweet that was flashing through her mind. *What does it take to wipe murder off the menu?* Dee Dee was right: it was a threat. *I have to tell Tom.*

"Secrets are married to lies," Pippa De Long lectured as she paced around the stage, waving her neon yellow scarf for emphasis. "Keep that in mind as you consider just what's at stake for your character." Then the tenacious director called for a fifteen-minute break. "I'm sure we'll all be sharper after a few refreshments." She glared at Eliza.

Eliza offered Pippa a nod and a conciliatory smile. Then she bounded off the stage, grabbed a Diet Pepsi from the vending machine and settled into one of the regal theater's fraying royal blue velvet seats. She tried to fix her mind on the script. Her character, Sandra, a celebrated and self-absorbed concert pianist, who easily surrendered her baby to her rival after her ex-husband's plane disappeared and he was presumed dead, surely had enough secrets to ruminate upon. Still Eliza's mind detoured back to real life strife.

The tweets were only part of the troubling cocktail that consumed Eliza. Jonas was M.I.A. Adelaide La Fontaine's departure date still remained up for grabs. And despite Nathaniel Miller's arrest, Eliza wasn't so sure the Deborah Attwater case had been solved. *One mystery at a time.* Eliza punched in Jonas' cell number. "Damn. I keep getting voicemail," she mumbled. "Where are you? It's been over a week. I thought you were on the way home. Call me. Okay? As soon as you get this." She regretted that last command. Just her luck: Jonas would call back right in the middle of rehearsal and Eliza would really catch Pippa's wrath. *Too bad*, she thought. She was getting nervous now. *About so many things.*

"Thanks for this," Colin O'Neal said, sidling up to Eliza, holding a half-eaten blackberry doughnut plucked from the box of assorted goodies she'd left on the snack table. "I hope I live up to expectations. I mean, I'm not exactly George Brent."

"Oh, you'll do," Eliza said, taking in her co-star's tall, trim frame, his amiable, if not quite handsome, features.

"So as our resident professional, how do think rehearsals are going?"

"A little rough around the edges, but we'll get there." Eliza had no business exuding confidence as she'd tripped over more lines than anyone else tonight.

"Keep plugging away, I guess." Colin licked powdered sugar off his lips. "Take my wife; she says everyone's got a vault of secrets. Just look at that gal—that Admissions honcho over at Quimby. Can you imagine the secrets that will spill out of her vault?"

"Like what?"

"All these affairs... I bet that professor's just the tip of the iceberg. And that business with the blackmail—or is it extortion? I always get the two mixed up."

"Blackmail? What are you talking about?"

"Just saw a piece on the *Grapevine*. Said *inside sources* reported she'd been getting threats to *expose* her."

Eliza sighed heavily. "Expose her over what?"

"Didn't say."

"Well, I'd take whatever you read on the *Grapevine* with a pound of salt." Not that Eliza put any stock into the trash scrawled across that hateful site, but she remembered Jonas had mentioned Deb fretting over threatening letters.

"You're probably right." Colin finished off his doughnut. "Anyway, I'm not so sure my wife's right. Remember when Geraldo opened Al Capone's safe on live TV? That's how empty my vault would be. So empty you could hear an echo." Colin laughed and just for a second Eliza detected a sneer slip across his earnest face.

Pippa clapped her hands. "Thespians! Your attention is required on the stage!"

Just then, Eliza's phone rang. *Perfect timing.* Jonas' number appeared.

"Hello," she answered in a hushed tone. "Jonas, what's going on?" But all she heard on the other end was a muffled crackle. And then the cold dial tone.

CHAPTER 20

Damn. Another voicemail. Where the hell is Jonas? Eliza was trying to keep her growing panic under control. But she kept calling: seven times last night, twice already this morning. All she got was voicemail. Okay, so she'd only left three messages, but surely he must have seen she'd called so many times. He had to realize how worried she was.

It was just passed ten in the morning now, and Midge had opened her Tuesday show with the jaunty Chris Montez hit "Call Me." *Wow, she's good*, Eliza thought. She always thought her pal was a little psychic.

"Oh, God, not another one," Dee Dee blurted out, spying Eliza clutching her phone as the girl swung through the kitchen and back behind the counter.

"What? Oh, no, not *that*." Eliza shook her phone, placed it on a Gary Cooper placemat on the counter. *That's all I need. Another threatening tweet.* And, yes, she couldn't help it; she was now thinking of them as threats. "It's Jonas. I can't get a hold of him."

"Yeah, we were wondering what happened to him. I mean, it's fun to skip a class. But three?"

"Oh, right; I forgot. You're taking his course. So what do they do? Just cancel for the week?"

"Well, we only meet twice a week. So last week was a no go. But yesterday, the TA chick showed a movie. That *Mary, Marcy Marlene* or whatever it's called. A funky little film about some mixed-up girl who falls into a cult and how weird her life is when she tries to go home."

"Did she say anything about why he wasn't there?"

Dee Dee shook her head, spun the cap off a bottle of Snapple raspberry iced tea. "Nah, she just said something like he was 'unavoidably detained.' I think that's what she said, but she mumbles. When she talks. God, she's a weird chick."

"Weird like how?'

"I don't know. She rarely says anything. She mostly just gives the evil eye to all the girls in class, especially the pretty ones. Think she's got the hots for Jonas. But who doesn't?" Dee Dee tittered nervously. "Sorry."

"No need." Eliza laughed, but there was a sigh residing inside it that made an odd little noise. "That's his lot in life. And he knows how to handle himself." Now she only hoped Jonas' life hadn't taken him someplace he couldn't manage.

"You think something happened to him?"

"I don't know what's going on." Eliza got off her stool and started puttering around the working end of the counter, checking the placemats, napkins, ketchup bottles. The lunch rush was less than an hour away. "He's a man of the world. He can handle almost anything. I just wish he'd call."

"You're sweet, you know that?"

"What? Where's this sentimentality coming from all of a sudden?"

"No, I mean it's like you're worried about him but you're also trying to pretend you're not. Like you want to protect me." Dee Dee blushed a bit as she wiped down the counter. "But you don't have to. I'm not some innocent little waif."

"I know."

"I'm just saying, if you need me... well, I'm here, that's all. I can have your back." Dee Dee blushed a bit more, her face turning a deep pink hue Eliza had never seen on the girl before. "Corny, huh?"

"Not at all. I appreciate it."

Midge segued into the Rolling Stones' "Mother's Little Helper," and Dee Dee burst out laughing. "That's just what Lois needs. A serious chill pill."

"What's her major maladjustment these days?"

"Oh, she's off the chain. On and on about this business at Quimby. I mean, yeah, okay, it's horrible what happened to Ms. Attwater and everything. Even worse, that Professor Miller was arrested. And I'm sure he didn't do it. He's too nice."

"You know him?"

"Yeah, I took English Comp with him when I transferred. My grades from Conn were so bad I had to re-enroll in some freshman classes. He was so great. He was really the one who gave me my confidence back."

"That's nice to hear. They said he was a popular professor."

"One of the best. And a lot of girls had crushes on him, too. Believe it or not. I mean he's not sexy like Jonas or anything. And I guess he's a slob. But he has—–I don't know—this sort of charisma, I guess. Anyway, he's too nice, too good, you know? Even if he was having a fling or whatever with Ms. Attwater. I mean, everyone knows he has something going with his TA almost every year. And last year's was a whack job… or at least that was the story going around campus. And he never killed any of *them*."

"I don't think he did it either." Eliza sighed. *It was curious*, Eliza thought, how both Deborah Attwater and Nathaniel Miller seemed to have been sexually insatiable people with the magnetism to lure lovers in.

Dee Dee checked the Soup Opera Twitter feed on her phone. "No new *love* tweets, thank God." Then she tweeted:

@SoupOpera: Catch of the Day: Lobster Bisque #KillerCuisine.

"You think that's still okay, right?" She flashed her phone at Eliza. "The *Killer Cuisine* part, I mean? With everything going on?"

"Yeah, I think we're good." Eliza smiled. She didn't have the psychic energy to add innocuous phrases like *killer cuisine* to the growing load of things to fret over.

"At least Lois has been in a better mood since that Adelaide La Fontaine lady checked in."

So happy Adelaide's presence has elevated someone's mood around here. "Yeah, they seem like two peas in a pod."

"And now her husband—what's his name? Curious George? Anyway, Lois thinks he's so cool, too. She actually called him—get this—" Dee Dee worked the rabbit ears air quotes: 'The sexiest dreamboat to hit town in decades.'" Dee Dee shook her head, rolled her eyes. "I mean *dreamboat*? Like what century are we in?"

"High praise is high praise."

"And now she's determined to get them back together. Can you imagine my mother as a matchmaker?"

"You never know." Eliza was hoping Lois could work some magic and get them both out of town with the same alacrity she had for annoying people.

"Either that or she'll go after him herself. Now that could be fun to watch."

Eliza stiffened, then nodded as the melodic Soup Opera chimes signaled the lunch shift was about to begin. "Hi there! You guys are early," Eliza said. A pair of regulars: two gals who worked down the street at the travel agency, grabbed a booth.

Eliza's phone rang. She spied Jonas' number, shot a pleading look in Dee Dee's direction.

"I got this," Dee Dee said as she approached the women with menus.

"Jonas? Where the hell are you?"

"No, lady. You've got the wrong number." It wasn't Jonas. It was an unfamiliar voice—flat and gravely—and she couldn't tell if it was coming from a man or a woman.

"What? But this is his... this is Jonas' number. And you called me."

"I know. I called to tell you to stop calling, lady."

"What? Who are you? How do you have this phone?"

"Don't call here again. Do you hear me, lady? Jonas doesn't live here anymore."

CHAPTER 21

"Jonas is missing!" Eliza blurted as she burst into Tom's office at the Goodship Police Station.

"What? What's going on?" Tom rose from behind his formidable desk, went to Eliza, gave her a hug and ushered her into the sturdy dark green leather arm chair in front of his desk. He dashed into the lobby, returned quickly with a glass of water he'd filled for her at the cooler. As he handed it to Eliza, he could see she was still shaking and there was sheer panic in her eyes.

"Relax a minute, sweetheart." Tom offered reassurance as he stroked her shoulder. "When you're ready, tell me what happened."

And after catching her breath and a few sips of water, she did. Eliza spilled it all. The Jonas saga: everything from what was supposed to be a weekend trip to San Francisco and the ten mysterious days that followed with only one brief call, interrupted by a bad connection; the voluminous unanswered voice mail messages; all culminating in that ominous call, earlier that day, from the stranger with Jonas' phone instructing her to stop calling. "Jonas doesn't live here anymore. That sounds threatening, right?"

Tom remained calm, focusing on Eliza without passing judgment or showing emotion. "Let's not get ahead of ourselves here. Maybe he just lost the phone."

"Jonas?" Eliza shook her head. "How do you just lose a phone? Jonas? Come on; he's not careless."

And then she launched into the Twitter rant. She wasn't going to; honestly, she didn't want to go anywhere near it. Not now. But earlier, while she was sitting in the police station parking lot, trying to compose herself, rehearsing her Jonas spiel, trying to rehearse calm, she just couldn't resist. No, she had to grab a glance at the feed. And there it was. Another nasty tweet.:

@EAPsLament @SoupOpera Time is ticking on the Tell Tale Tart! Who's got you covered #BaileyBarnes?

And then another:

@EAPsLament @Soup Opera: Stew in ur own juices, #BaileyBarnes! Ur final course will be served soon.

So now they were popping up faster. And two now from the same handle: @EAPsLament. *Creepy.*

If it had only been one, maybe, just maybe she could have waited to tell Tom. But she let it all out in one rambling gush of anxiety. She must have sounded like a complete hysterical fool. She knew she did, but she also knew Tom wouldn't be dismissive the way, say, Charlie Rosencrantz might or Detective Duckheimer surely would. For one thing, he loved her. And for another, he knew she wasn't readily given to hysterics. And while he may have been loath to admit it, and he certainly never encouraged it, he knew Eliza had very sharp instincts.

Tom nodded, smiled warmly. "So that explains why you've been checking your phone."

"So you noticed?"

"Are you kidding? I'd have to be comatose not to have seen you." Tom shook his head. "You were checking it like a compulsive gambler into a bookie for fifty large on football Sunday."

"But you didn't say anything."

Tom smiled. Eliza nodded, acknowledging and finally appreciating his ability to take everything in, his patience to let people tell what they needed to tell in their own time.

She showed him the two latest tweets on her phone.

"I can see why you're disturbed," Tom said, his tone measured, his countenance contained. "But it's probably just a prank. A misguided, overzealous fan."

"Maybe, but they seem to be getting, I don't know, creepier. More threatening, and they're coming more frequently." Eliza was breathing heavily. "I mean, when will it end?"

"Did you save the others?"

"No, I couldn't. They just disappeared... evaporated into thin air after they.... he... she... whoever, changed the Twitter handle. The last two are the first ones to come from the same handle. @EAPsLament. Whatever that means." Eliza shook her head, adding with a guilty lilt, "But Dee Dee and Sam saw them all." As if Tom might not have believed her? *Come on; of course, he believes me.*

"They may look like they vanished, but everything in cyberspace is forever. It's stored somewhere or floating around the Internet. We just have to know how to find it." Eliza was reassured by Tom's calm and his tech savvy. "You remember how you tracked down the *Goodship Grapevine* domain last summer? We can try and at least trace these tweets back to the IP address that sent them."

"Okay." Eliza started to feel better. She wasn't alone anymore. *Haven't been for while.* "What about Jonas?"

"Not sure," Tom said, working hard to conceal his concern. "Write down his number for me and we'll see if we can trace that, too." He handed Eliza an index card and she jotted it down.

"Sit tight. We'll work on it." Tom put his arm around Eliza's shoulders.

"Thank you," she whispered. And then the tears bubbled out, a stream of anxiety and relief.

"It's okay, sweetheart." Tom hugged her, his tight, comforting grasp filling her with love. "I'm just glad you finally told me."

"Chief?" Tom's secretary intruded by way of the intercom. "I know you're busy, but there's a woman in the lobby to see you. She's says it's a matter of *extreme urgency.*"

"Okay, Barb, I'll be out in a minute."

But the woman's familiar wave of pungent liberally doused fragrance arrived before her brazen entrance. "No need I'll come to you." Adelaide swung into the office, the lithe and infuriating dance of an entitled soloist. "What have I interrupted here? A nooner of sorts, Doodle? Didn't know you had it in you." She smiled.

Tom repelled by her seductive attempt at a kiss, backed away.

"What's this about? What can I do for you *now*, Adelaide?" Tom's tone was now stern, the tenderness he'd displayed to Eliza only a moment before had evaporated, Eliza knew, more permanently than those elusive tweets. His patience with the one who got away had finally run out.

"Well, Doodle, it seems I may be in a spot of trouble Just a smidge, I'm sure, but…"

"But what? What sort of trouble are you in?"

Both Tom and Eliza looked at the doorway as two somber looking men lurked in.

"I'm not exactly sure, Doodle. You better ask the FBI."

****

"I'll tell you one thing: I'm not breaking rocks in the hot sun like Martha Stewart or some skanky reality TV chickadee." Adelaide's charm was fading fast. "Not over *that* damn black book. And you can take that to the bank, Georgie."

The scene had unfolded so fast, Eliza didn't know what to make of it all. She'd been hurriedly ushered out of Tom's office and asked to wait in the austere Goodship Police Station lobby. So there she sat, affixed to a stiff grey chair, staring at the industrial grey tweed carpet. Tom hung back in the office, Adelaide insisting her *Doodle* sit with her until her attorney arrived.

"If you'd just handed that thing over when I asked you, we wouldn't be in this fix." George was fuming. He'd apparently been pacing the police station parking lot until Adelaide had waved him in.

Eliza mused once again about the sound-proofing, or lack thereof, as she heard dribs and drabs of the so-called interrogation. When the voices were low, the conversation was muffled. But when they were elevated, she could hear words like *embezzlement, extortion, bribery* and *brothel.*

One of the FBI agents asked something about government contracts. Another asked about concealing names of officials. "Are you holding on to documents for personal gain? Or to extort money from any official?"

She couldn't hear the answers. If there were any. Eliza suspected Adelaide was smart enough to clam up. And Glorious Georgie had to be pretty savvy, too. Something juicy, she figured, was contained in that book. Adelaide had been holding on to it, presumably, as leverage in their divorce. Georgie had tried to wrangle it back at a bargain price, no doubt. Neither had bargained on the FBI wanting to get their hands on it.

"Do either of you know a Belle LaRue, also known as Lady LaRue. Real name Mary Johanson?"

"Want to take that one, Georgie?"

"Not particularly, darlin.' Let's wait for Avery."

"Are you invoking?"

"Take it to the bank, G-Man." Adelaide sounded chipper. Eliza marveled at the aging beauty queen's ability to slip into the poise and lingo of a 1940's *film noir* mol.

And with that, the interrogation was over. Tom's office door opened and Adelaide and Georgie emerged––both smiling, now holding hands as they rushed to the exit.

Tom and the FBI agents came out next, all looking wrung out and slightly perplexed. Their reactions amused Eliza. Although she hadn't been privy to the whole thing, she'd pieced together enough to know that whatever Georgie, and by extension Adelaide, may have been suspected of, they surely weren't about to simply spill their guts. Not without talking to a lawyer and making a deal that, at least in Adelaide's case, didn't involve spending one minute in the Big House.

"Ready for lunch?" Eliza asked as Tom approached.

"No, sorry, honey." He looked serious. "I have to go over a few things with the agents." The two men were standing by Tom's office door.

"Okay, I understand."

"I think they may be able to help with those other matters."

"Oh, good." Eliza clutched Tom's hand as she rose from the chair.

He kissed her lightly on the cheek. "I'll call you later. Don't worry."

"Not as much anyway."

CHAPTER 22

Eliza didn't have time to digest the startling Adelaide and Glorious Georgie La Fontaine developments. By the time she got back to Soup Opera, the lunch rush was in full swing and rumors in the Deborah Attwater murder investigation were pouring in faster than bowls of her ever popular lobster bisque were pouring out.

"He made bail. Can you believe? Lois Danziger, in all her hysterical glory, was nervously nibbling on a turkey and cranberry flatbread at the counter. "I mean what does that mean? They don't have a solid case against Nathaniel Miller all of a sudden? Maybe they think someone else did it?"

"Don't be such a ninny," Miriam Sussman snipped with her signature bitter-lemon diplomacy. "It just means the slob landed a top attorney." Miriam waved a copy of the *Goodship Citizen Gazette*. "Andrew Gregorian." She snorted. The high profile criminal defense attorney, a cable TV fixture, who flaunted his tactics representing celebrity clients had signed on to Nathaniel Miller's case. First order of business: getting the shamed professor's bail reduced and waltzing him out of the Westchester County jail.

"Gregorian may have pulled that rabbit out of his legal hat because the case is so thin, " Midge offered, as she grabbed a potato chip form Lois' plate. "My money's on the soon to be ex-Mrs. Miller."

Eliza shot an inquisitive look in Midge's direction. With everything going on—including Midge's precarious position as an early suspect—Eliza hadn't had time to mull over the case with her best pal. So it was funny to find them both on the same suspicious page. Or maybe not. Maybe the cops were just ignoring the obvious. Then again, maybe they had good reason. After all, Eliza and Midge weren't privy to all the evidence. For all they knew, Cynthia could have had an airtight alibi.

"Well she's got some infamous temper." Midge smiled. "Not that I should talk."

"Guess there's no escaping." Eliza could hear the distinct voice before Sweet Lorraine Dresser made her way to the Soup Opera counter.

"Riding solo today?" Eliza asked as the detective grabbed a stool next to Midge.

"Want to get my head out of the case. And into a big bowl of your lobster bisque."

"Coming right up," Eliza said. "Big bisque. Stat!" she called into the kitchen; could almost feel Dee Dee's eye roll scorch her back.

"Gosh, I remember when this used to be Smithee's Apothecary."

"Really? You're from Goodship?"

"Born and raised. Used to sit at a counter like this— well, not as fancy schmanzy—and fill up on chocolate malts and bottomless banana splits. Yep, I'm that old."

"I never knew you were a native," Midge perked up. "So how did you manage the escape?"

"First husband. Snuck me across state lines. Right into Connecticut." Sweet Lorraine let out her signature cough-bark-rasp-laugh, "The marriage didn't take, but I stayed on."

"Ah, a love affair with the Nutmeg State," Eliza said. "I can see that. The quaint charm is very alluring."

"More of a marriage of convenience. I got the cushy Greenwich condo in the divorce."

"Greenwich, huh?" Miriam Sussman raised her eyebrows. "Now that's the place to commit murder."

The counter crowd darted shocked looks at the crank.

"No, she's right," Sweet Lorraine laughed. "They still have a few unsolved murders on the books. Maybe when I retire I'll take up local cold cases as a hobby."

"Oh, for God's sake. Enough chit-chat about unsolved ancient cases. What about this one?" Lois' face was flushed with a daunting beet red blush. "Did you know Nathaniel Miller made bail? Why didn't you quash it?"

"Quash what? Bail?" Lorraine emitted a sound, but it was more snide grunt than joyous laugh.

"Well, yeah. Maybe you feel comfortable with a maniac murderer on the loose, but I sure don't."

"First of all, the law does not recognize Mr. Miller as a murderer. He's merely a murder suspect."

"Oh, come on. You're not going to go into all that 'innocent until proven guilty' nonsense, are you?"

"Not if you consider The Constitution nonsense."

"You know what I mean. You didn't arrest him because you thought he was innocent, right?"

"Right. But everyone is entitled to a trial. Every suspect, every defendant has rights. We can't just toss them like yesterday's soup *du jour*."

"God forbid," Eliza said.

"Okay, but why do you think they reduced bail?" Lois asked. "Maybe the judge thinks the evidence is flimsy. Maybe you have another suspect in mind?"

"Pure conjecture," Miriam sniffed. "Where do you get this uncorroborated junk?"

Lois, now off her stool, was standing, hands on hips, anxiously kicking the bottom of Lorraine's stool with her right foot which was uncharacteristically encased in a bright green high-top sneaker.

Dee Dee popped out of the kitchen, spied her mom, and slithered back.

"I can't speak for the judge," Lorraine said, her eyes riveted to Lois' flashy footwear. "And as for our investigation: I certainly cannot comment on any potential suspects or developments." Lorraine's professional tone may have impressed Eliza, but she found it rather disappointing too.

"They're all the same," Lois said. "Always putting up that great big blue wall of silence."

Lorraine erupted into laughter. It was the loudest bark-cough-rasp-laugh Eliza had ever heard emanate from the detective. "Don't ask me why, but I like you, lady," Lorraine managed to say to Lois. "You got great style too. Tell me: where did you get those nifty kicks?"

"These?" Lois groused as she raised her right foot slightly and twisted it around. "A gag gift, but my feet are killing me. I overdid it at the gym." Then in hushed tones: "And I have a small bunion issue."

"Ah, all too familiar," Lorraine said, glancing at her own purple sneakers.

"Well, anyway…someone leaked something. It's all over the latest Sage Wisdom column on the *Grapevine*." Lois was back to business.

"Sage Wisdom?" Lorraine's face fell. She shook her head, the auburn shrub—today bifurcated by a blue and black blotchy scarf that didn't exactly go with her fuchsia tunic or her lime green Capri pants—barely moving. "Don't believe *anything* you read in that column." Lorraine quickly reconciled the check and dashed off without much fanfare.

"Something's up," Lois said. "That reaction. You saw that. She knows something. Just watch. This thing is not wrapped up." Lois glared at Miriam. "I don't care who says it is." Then she paid her bill and pranced out of Soup Opera as if she'd scored some elusive victory.

"Ninny," Miriam said. "Always was. Always will be." Then Miriam vacated her stool, and she, too, reconciled her bill.

"Finally figured out how to clear a room," Midge quipped.

"Yeah, but what'd we do exactly?"

"Got me." The gals laughed.

The Soup Opera chimes signaled Tom's entrance. "Hi! Sorry about earlier."

"No worries, Chief. But you missed all the action."

Dee Dee sprung through the kitchen door again. "Well, maybe not all the action."

Eliza took one look at the girl's face, drained of levity. And she knew.

"No, don't..."

"Sorry, but there's..."

"Another one? Already?"

Eliza looked, then showed Tom and Midge the latest tweet on Dee Dee's iPhone.

@EAPsLament @SoupOpera Drown in ur soup Bailey Barnes. But ur not the only one. Bail is no Get Out Of Jail Free Card #MurderersMustPay

CHAPTER 23

"She burned someone big time. Or else she iced him," Colin O'Neal told Eliza as the two sat on the Goodship Community Playhouse stage Wednesday evening, waiting for rehearsal to begin.

"Excuse me?"

"That Deborah Attwater woman," Colin said. "I told you she steamed a lot of people with her seductive ways. That prof wasn't the only one. Hell, looks like the cops have their eyes on someone else anyway."

"Really? What makes you think so?"

"It's all over the *Goodship Grapevine*."

Eliza shook her head. *Figures. God, that Grapevine is still the same.* Even after Miriam Sussman had sold it to Local Media One, the company that owned *The Goodship Citizen Gazette,* Eliza figured it was still just an unreliable gossip site in business for the ad click bait. "I told you; you shouldn't believe everything you read."

"Maybe not. But I can make up my own mind." Colin beamed that boastful big lottery winner's look of someone about to spill some seriously salacious beans. "I can tell you firsthand how she lured people in. Then she'd throw 'em away like yesterday's fish without even bothering to wrap them in old newspaper."

"Wait... What? You knew her? You knew Deb Attwater?"

"Well, I wouldn't say that exactly. Don't think anyone knew *knew* her. But I got a pretty good glimpse for a few months when I re-hauled their website last fall. She had this young kid sniffing around her like some lost puppy dog. Imagine, a cougar chick like that leading a young stud around."

Eliza was flummoxed. And, for the moment, rendered speechless. Colin hadn't mentioned his close encounters with Deb Attwater Monday night when he had speculated on all the secrets that would pour out of her *crazy vault*. She wondered if the *young stud* Colin had referred to was that guy Geo from the Admissions Office; Eliza had witnessed the aftermath of a tryst between him and Deborah Attwater shortly before her murder. Maybe he had stronger feelings for Deb than the insatiable Admissions honcho could reciprocate. Or maybe Colin had something to hide. *Maybe Colin had been one of Deborah Attwater's pathetic discards.*

"I'll tell you one thing," Colin continued. "I don't think that professor did it. Never thought so."

"Why?" Eliza didn't think so either, but she figured she might as well pump Colin for his so-called *firsthand* insights.

"Well, they were cut from the same cloth. Both users. Unsentimental sexual vipers." Colin's eyes grew wide.

"Wow, that's a pretty harsh assessment."

"Call it like I see it." Colin flashed that snide little sneer that had unnerved Eliza the other night.

"Oh, dear." Wendy Orenstein was making her way down the wide royal blue and gold print theatre stairs, negotiating her enormous overstuffed tote dropping toddler breadcrumbs as she made her journey. She had already retrieved a blue and yellow polka-dotted blanket, a stuffed elephant and a box of Animal Crackers. Now a small pillow, a sippy cup and a Mickey Mouse all tumbled out in rapid and awkward succession.

"Holy Crepe Suzettes!" Wendy blurted in exasperation as she went about gathering up the latest escapees, only to have a toy dinosaur and a pair of fruit punch juice boxes drop out of her unwieldy goodie bag. "Crepe Suzettes… oh, so sorry." Another two stairs and another item—this time a colorful ball and oh, look, Mickey Mouse again. "*Crepe Suzettes* already!" Wendy shouted as she re-loaded the tote and inched closer to the stage.

"Jeez! Get a load of this," Colin said to Eliza, squinting his usually amiable brown eyes. "I mean *Crepe Suzettes*? Come on. Good thing you agreed to play Sandra. That one would infuse the part with all the depth of a 1950's Doris Day movie."

Eliza winced. "I know you didn't mean to, but you just gave Wendy a big compliment. Doris Day—and all those classic romantic comedies—are underrated," Eliza admonished. "They're genius. And they still hold up."

"Whatever you say. You're the professional here." Colin smiled, but his eyes were cold.

Something was off. Eliza didn't know what. But something about Colin, his reactions, and the way he'd been slow to reveal his personal connection to Deb Attwater told her he wasn't quite as affable as he'd seemed. His protestations to the contrary, Eliza wondered if Colin's own vault contained some serious and intriguing secrets. She'd have to try and open it with careful precision.

Pippa De Long breezed to the stage. "The company will assemble, please!" she commanded, waving her purple print scarf. "Tonight, we dig deeper."

Yes, Eliza thought. *Much deeper.*

CHAPTER 24

Eliza's sleuth wheels spun her into maximum overdrive on the ride home from rehearsal. By the time she pulled Eddie's old Jeep into the driveway, she'd already made rock solid cases against both the soon-to-be ex Mrs. Miller and Eliza's enigmatic co-star Colin O'Neal. Of course, the cases were fueled largely by motivations and some of those she had to concede may have been manufactured by a former soap actress's wayward imagination. Still she was excited enough; she considered calling Midge to mull over the suspect list.

But that snoop sister gab fest would have to wait. Before she got to her front door, a familiar bark beckoned Eliza's attention. Her neighbor Simon Teague was walking his boisterous Airedale, Montgomery. Or more aptly: the dog was walking Simon, who appeared more harried than usual. And infirmed. The middle-aged divorced dad's left arm was bundled under a sling and his ragged red and purple Madras plaid Bermuda shorts were sagging, lending him an odd preppie clown at the country club veneer.

"Hey, Monty, easy!" Simon pleaded with his companion, as the dog pulled the leash in Eliza's direction.

"Hi, Monty." Eliza smiled, hesitantly petting the dog. His frenetic behavior had always reinforced her feline proclivities. "Hi, Simon, what happened there? Monty take you for a trip?"

"Not this time." Simon shook his head, pulling tighter on the leash, which seemed to appease Monty for the moment. "Took the boys to a water park in New Jersey. Let's just say I got on the wrong side of a very oversized slide."

"Oh, dear. So sorry."

"Well, the kids had fun." Simon smiled. "And that's the only thing that really matters, right?"

Eliza nodded and smiled. "Guess so," she offered, but by then Monty had stepped on the canine accelerator and master and companion were half way down the street faster than if Midge had driven them around the block.

Hitchcock greeted her at the door. Quick to grab and snuggle the corpulent bundle of affection, Eliza knew the cat had ulterior motives. *Food. Glorious food.*

"Sorry, no sale, Hitch." Eliza sighed. She usually gave into the pleading purrs, but with another vet visit hovering like a dark, high calorie cloud, it was a no-go. "The kitchen is closed."

Of course, that was a lie. After taking a quick shower, Eliza wound up in the kitchen huddled over the island, eating a rare bowl of leftover Soup Opera Manhattan clam chowder. There were scenes to go over, and suspects to review. And, for now anyway, Hitchcock was curled up on the sunken sofa in the living room.

In *The Great Lie,* Eliza's character Sandra agrees to allow her nemesis Maggie, who'd married her ex shortly before he took off and went missing on a secret government mission, to raise her baby. She had her hot shot concert career to consider, and the baby would get an honorable name and his rightful place in society, something that was a bigger deal in the 1940's than today. Although in certain circles such things still mattered. Still, Sandra was an anomaly. Most mothers wouldn't simply surrender their babies for the sake of convenience or even status.

A cartoon light bulb flashed in Eliza's mind. Most parents would do almost anything to ensure their children's happiness. *That's what really matters.* Isn't that what Simon Teague had just said? A parent's passion, not a lover's, may have propelled the murderous fury that brought down Deborah Attwater.

The phone rang. It was Midge.

"I have two words for you," Midge said, chipper now, back to her old self. "Henry Mancini"

"Okay, I'll play. 'Dead movie composers' for 400, Alex?"

Midge snickered. "A different Henry Mancini. This one's an accountant from Dover, Delaware."

"And what exactly are we doing with this accountant from Delaware?"

"Suspecting him of murder." Midge paused. Eliza figured this was where the suspenseful movie music, something preferably by Bernard Herrmann, would be inserted in the soundtrack playing in her pal's head. "The murder of Deborah Attwater."

"Okay.... Who is he?"

"He's that incensed father. You remember; you were there. He's the guy you saw at *Mucho Gusto* yelling and waving bread and God knows what else at Deb Attwater and Nathaniel Miller. Remember the guy with the oboe-playing son? You know, the night Gus got a two-act dinner theater show for free."

"Oh, okay. So?"

"So he made his big star turn scene the night before Deb Attwater's murder."

"Yeah, I remember. So how does that make him a suspect?"

"He stopped by her office Friday, too." Midge sounded impatient with Eliza. "They had a huge fight. Witnesses were in the outer office. He really wanted his son to get accepted to Quimby."

"Yeah, well a lot of people wanted *their* kids to get in. It wasn't too long ago when a certain occasionally hot-tempered mom found herself in the jackpot seat."

"I know. Thanks for the reminder."

"Sorry, I didn't mean anything by it. It's just not a lot there to pin the murder on him."

"That's because you jumped the gun... so to speak."

"So what else you got?"

"So how about a stack of threatening letters? E-mails for weeks, one or two snail mails, too, I think. But don't hold me to it."

"Wait. What? This Mancini guy was threatening her?" Jonas' concern over the threatening letters he'd dismissed ran through her mind. Now Deb was dead and Jonas was still missing in action. "That could be big."

"That's what I've been saying."

"So where'd you get this anyway?" Eliza tried to conceal her skepticism, but she knew it oozed through her voice.

"Sage Wisdom."

Now there was no hiding it. Eliza let out a disdainful sigh. "Oh, here we go."

"What does that mean?" Midge was prickly now.

"Isn't that that new column on *The Goodship Grapevine*?"

"Yeah, so? They have sources."

"I'm sure Perez Hilton and Cindy Adams are shaking in their shoes."

"Okay, Cynical Sally, try this on for size: he checked into the Goodship Inn for nearly a week. And Lois said he made a commotion in the lobby about a discrepancy on his bill."

"If that was enough to make an arrest, you'd have to place the whole hotel on permanent lockdown," Eliza scoffed.

"Okay, but get this: Lois said she also saw him working out in the gym two, three times a day."

"Another smoking gun." Eliza snuck a now half cold slurp of soup.

"It might be," Midge snipped. "He was lifting weights. Beefing up to wield that snow globe, no doubt."

"Oh, now I get it. Better call Charlie Rosencrantz and Lorraine Dresser. Bet they'll put out an APB ASAP." Eliza laughed.

Midge slammed the phone down. Just then Hitchcock sauntered in, his hazel eyes pleading.

"The best I can do is freshen your water, sir." She refilled the cat's water dish. He sniffed around the bowl, let out a scornful meow and waddled away.

"Everyone hates me tonight," Eliza muttered. Figuring she may as well go full tilt tizzy, she pulled out her phone and checked the Soup Opera Twitter notification page.

@EAPsLament Midnight Dreary? Ponder this weak & weary. You will escape #nevermore.

With little hope of a speedy visit from the sandman, Eliza fell into the sunken sofa and, with the remote in her shaky hand, trolled the TV for late night distraction. She landed on *Our Very Own*, an old movie with Ann Blyth as a teenager who discovers she'd been adopted, and all the emotions surrounding her attempt to reconnect with her birth mother fueled the melodrama of a simplistic and sentimental early 50's tear-jerker. It was entertaining, but it wasn't the cinematic Ambien Eliza needed.

CHAPTER 25

Eliza spent the night talking herself off the Twitter ledge. Those intimidating tweets came in fast and furious. Ten in two hours, repetitive veiled and not-so-veiled threats. A few laced with literary references, a few soupy tweets drowned in overused food clichés. Murder had been on the menu since this whole business started. And it wasn't about to be wiped off the Specials Board just by wishing it away. If anything, things were intensifying. The whack job tweeter was becoming more and more impatient. And seriously unhinged.

@EAPsLament @SoupOpera Midnight Dreary paradise compared to deep, dark fate that awaits. #nevermore already!

Before eleven, shortly after spying that first tweet of the night, Eliza called Tom, but Bert told her he'd been called to Washington for an emergency meeting. "Hush hush, top secret," Bert said. "Never happened in my day." Eliza didn't want to alarm Bert, although she knew the retired police chief was just as compassionate as his son, and still as sharp.

Since sleep was an elusive option, she trolled the @EAPsLament page. The bio line : WAITING TO STRIKE summed it up. But Eliza wasn't the creep's only target. He, she—whoever—also took aim at, among others: Donald Trump, Rachel Ray, and @AdoptionConnection. But other than Eliza, the most prominent target was @QuimbyConfidential.

A barrage of tweets, all with a familiar ring, pelted the college feed.

@EAPsLament @QuimbyConfidential Think you're smarter than cops? Catch me if you can. #MurdererInYourMidst.

So now it was an interactive game the nutso was playing. Eliza started to wonder if engaging the tweeter might be the only way to stop the menacing momentum. But she didn't want to do anything without talking it over with Tom. She texted Tom—told him to call her in the morning. And by that, of course, she meant the civilized morning. It was after three when she finally stowed her phone in the kitchen cabinet, stashed way back behind boxes of Special K Red Berries and Carr's water crackers, all the way in the back behind her old vintage miniature gum ball machine and a gravy boat shaped like a fish her eccentric Aunt Maura had presented with much fanfare on her wedding day. She wanted to resist the temptation of the desperate glance. She hoped against every ounce of hope that she could catch a few hours of sleep

And somehow she'd drifted into slumber. On that darn sunken sofa. That's where Hitchcock was circling, purring, threatening to pounce, presumably on Thursday morning. The sun was glaring through the blinds as Eliza awoke, startled, achy, groping for a clock or watch. But ejecting herself from that sunken mushy pit was the first order of groggy morning business. She managed to stagger into the kitchen, moving in slow motion, feeling like a contorted pretzel. She spied the wall clock; 9:17 winked back like a hapless sigh of a guilty hangover. But rather than remnants of a gleeful celebration or tortured bender, it was anxiety (and snatches of uncomfortable sleep) that had muddled her head. Before she could muster the adrenaline to put her oh-so-late rear in gear, she heard a familiar, but muffled ping emanate from the cabinet above the granite island. *Her cell phone.* She navigated the boxes and obstacles and rescued her captor. She figured it must be Dee Dee. But no, it was Tom. She'd just missed the call. He left a voicemail. "Hello? Okay, you're probably in the shower. Almost home. Stay there. I'm coming over. If you're already at Soup Opera, call and I'll meet you there. But I kinda think it would be better at your place.... But either way... it's okay... don't worry. I have some good news. Love you. See you soon."

She quickly called in. Dee Dee answered cheerfully. "Things are fine. Pretty busy, but under control."

"So sorry. I'm on my way," Eliza stammered.

"What for?"

"I'm beyond late." Eliza was now stumbling around her bedroom, fetching things out of her closet with—if there was such a thing—laconic urgency.

"No, you're not. Sam and I opened up today."

"Oh, right." Eliza pulled on a pair of jeans. "That was on the schedule?"

"Yeah. You okay? You sound a little... I don't know... off."

"Didn't sleep too well; that's all. But I'm okay." Eliza gingerly pulled a t-shirt over her stiff neck. "Actually, I may be a little later than I thought."

"Uh, okay. Like I said, everything's under control." Then to incoming customers, "Good morning...sure, grab a booth. I'll be right with you."

"Go do your thing, Thanks so much."

"Sure. Take your time." Before hanging up, Eliza heard rustling and Dee Dee blurted: "What?... You're kidding? Another one?"

"What's going on?" Eliza asked. "Is it another tweet?" But the only answer she got was the echo of the stark dial tone.

CHAPTER 26

@EAPsLament @SoupOpera Arise & crime. Scrambled motives. #Justice will be served!

After seeing the recent tweet, Eliza convinced herself that that was the source of Dee Dee's dismay. But she rushed around anyway. She put out fresh water and Science Diet low-cal food for the cats. Hitchcock was headed for the vet's scales and Tallulah wouldn't know the difference. She brushed on some make-up, grabbed her keys, and headed for the door. *Better make tracks*. Just in case some other ominous cloud had descended down upon Soup Opera. Before tossing the phone into her bag, she called Tom. "I've got to get to Soup Opera. See you there."

"Okay, but I'm here," Tom said.

She opened the door and there he stood. *Her guy*. Steady, sturdy, handsome Tom Santini. "So glad to see you, Tommy," Eliza said, as she almost fell into his arms for an embrace. And, yes, through all the turmoil of the past weeks: Deborah Attwater's murder, Midge, then Jonas as suspects, the crazy tweets, even the whole Adelaide La Fontaine business, Eliza had come to claim Tom as *her* guy. It wasn't just something she thought; it wasn't a tentative dating honorific. It was something she now felt deep down in her marrow. Without trying, without even expecting it, somehow her bond with Tom had strengthened through this arduous time.

"Let's go back inside. Just for a few minutes," Tom said, still holding her, guiding her into the kitchen.

They sat around the granite island on black high-backed stools that were as stiff as her sofa was squishy. She had, she realized, made some unfortunate furniture decisions. Then she half-laughed at herself for fretting over such a mundane detail. With everything hanging over them, there was still this domestic oasis. She filled glasses with Tom's favorite Arizona iced tea lemonade, and took in what he'd told her. The Washington trip was all about her—well, her mysterious and menacing tweeter.

"Really? You went all that way for me?" She was surprised, and then again she wasn't.

"Can't think of a better reason to visit the nation's capitol." Tom's smile was infused with reassurance and love.

"That's nice," she said, re-filling his glass. He looked exhausted; his beautiful azure eyes were rimmed with red. "But couldn't they tell you all of this over the phone?"

"Maybe, but I wanted to see firsthand what they'd uncovered. Plus it never hurts to show up in person." He let out a weary laugh. "Kind of underscores the urgency, if you know what I mean."

Eliza nodded. And Tom told her about the special FBI whiz with the special fine-tuned software that could track down almost anyone doing almost anything anywhere.

"Like I told you, once something's out over the Internet, on social media, wherever, it's out there forever."

"Okay, so how come they have such a hard time tracking terrorists?"

"Well, some of these guys, these terrorists, are savvy; they have encryption software that renders their communications untraceable." Tom sighed. "And the wannabes, the so-called radicalized recruits, can be rather elusive. Until…"

"Until they actually strike?"

"Yeah, I'm afraid so. But you'd be surprised at how many they can shut down, how many tragic events have been thwarted through chatter and leads."

"I guess things would be a lot worse without all the crackerjack tactics we never hear about."

"You bet," Tom said, putting his hand on top of hers. "Good thing your guy, gal, tweet person, isn't that cagey."

Tom told her about how the FBI hotshots had managed to trace the IP address where the @EAPsLament Twitter account was generated from. It was also where many—though not all—the tweets from that account had emanated.

"Brace yourself."

"What?" Eliza felt her face go flush.

Tom, seeing how stricken she looked, inched closer, held her hand tighter. "No, it's just, well I think the tweeter is local. The IP address was traced to a computer in the Quimby College library system."

"Oh, God. So he, whoever may really be after me? It's not just some prankster with lots of time on his hands?"

"Wait. Let's not get carried away."

The truth was Eliza wasn't shocked they were dealing with a local menace.

The tweet freak had, after all, also targeted the Quimby Confidential page. Eliza pulled up @EAPsLament's page on her phone and showed it to Tom.

@EAPsLament @QuimbyConfidential Asleep at the wheel? Cops veer in wrong lane. But has #justice already been served?

Tom perused the page, noting the number of tweets directed at @Soup Opera and @Quimby Confidential. "Seems to be a fifty-fifty split"

"Wait... you don't think there's a connection... between Deb Attwater's murder and this freak's obsession with me?"

Tom sighed. "Honey, please don't..."

"Okay, but maybe... it looks like he wants a confrontation. Maybe we could... I don't know... set up a trap or something."

"Not a good idea." Tom shook his head.

Just then Hitchcock waddled into the kitchen, pulling out all the stops on his pleading-purring routine.

The act was hard to resist; he looked so adorably pathetic. But Eliza just scooped him up in her arms. "No sale, pal," she said. "What's out is what's out. That's it. Until dinner."

She glanced at the clock. Almost ten. "I really got to get over to Soup Opera," she said without an ounce of enthusiasm.

Tom dismounted his stool and went to her side. With his arms around her (and her mushy mound of a cat) he said, "Don't worry, sweetheart. Please. Let the FBI take care of this."

"Okay, Tommy."

"Just don't let your soap opera imagination get out of control." He kissed her on the cheek. "It'll be okay, I promise."

Tallulah sauntered in. Her disdainful hiss propelled Hitchcock to bolt from Eliza's arms. And within seconds, they launched into a full blown catfight with water splashing and bits of dry food flying across the shiny hard wood floor.

"Go," Tom said as he sprung into action, cleaning up the feline debris. "I'll take care of this and let myself out." He jangled his pockets, indicating he had his key to her townhouse at the ready.

"Okay, thanks." Eliza gave Tom a sweet kiss on his stubbly cheek. "But maybe go upstairs and take a nap first. You look so tired, Tommy."

"Yeah, maybe," Tom said with a wistful smile. "I could get comfortable here."

Heading to the door, Eliza checked her phone and sprinted back to the kitchen. "I can't believe I almost forgot. What about Jonas? You said that FBI agent could track down his cell phone situation, too."

Tom grimaced, his shoulders sagged. "Not yet. But they're still working on it."

"Oh, okay." Eliza bristled, walked out into the pristine spring day. "Another dead end."

CHAPTER 27

Yolo Steinberg was missing.

That was the latest drama. But Eliza didn't get the story until the busy breakfast shift had wrapped and Dee Dee had dashed back to campus for a class. Sam gave Eliza the basics: The eccentric high profile prof hadn't been seen or heard from, it seems, for three days. And since she'd been slated to give the keynote at a big deal performance art conference in New York City the previous night, the entire Quimby campus seemed braced for more bad news.

"And now those Pixie Pastry girls are missing, too," Sam said as he readjusted his Mets cap, standing high above his bushy sandy mane.

"What? What happened to them?"

Sam shrugged. "Don't know. They never showed this morning." So breakfast had been running on day-old doughnut fumes and Michelle's brownies. "We practically sold out of the double fudge and blondies."

"Well, Michelle will be thrilled," Eliza said, assessing the pathetic pastry dome. "But what's their story?"

"Maybe it's a real life *The Leftovers.*"

"Excuse me?"

"That HBO show where... I don't know... something like a third of the population just vanishes on the same day. I guess it's supposed to be like a Rapture deal."

"Oh, right." Eliza arched her brow. "But I'm pretty sure there's a more earthly explanation."

Back for the lunch shift, Dee Dee swirled through the bustling eatery like a whirling dervish hepped up on Red Bull. So it wasn't until after two when they were both in the kitchen, tending the diminishing soup vats and starting sandwich prep for the commuter dinner crowd that the girl let all her anxiety gush like a geyser with a promiscuous spout.

"I mean, come on. One AWOL professor is bad enough. But two? Not to mention the dead Admissions honcho." Dee Dee stomped around the kitchen with such lumbering anxious anger she practically transformed her kicky pink Keds into combat boots. "Wait 'til my mother gets wind of this. I mean she's already off the chain."

"That's hardly a barometer"

"I thought you'd be more upset, too," Dee Dee said. "I mean it's not like Jonas has turned up. Aren't you *still worried* about him?"

"Of course." Eliza turned the ladle in the lobster bisque vat with such vigor she actually splattered herself with pot dregs. *Another dead end.* Wasn't that what Tom had said about the FBI's investigation or interest in Jonas' disappearance? No, wait. Those were Eliza's words. Tom had said they were still working on it. *Don't get carried away.*

"It's just... well, maybe Professor Steinberg got called away. Maybe she has a sick relative or some other family crisis. Maybe she had to rush somewhere in the middle of the night."

"So she wouldn't call someone? She wouldn't let people on campus or that conference know? She's been talking about that all semester."

"Wait! You know here?" Eliza ran a damp paper towel across her soiled apron. "Do you have a class with Yolo Steinberg, too?"

"Yeah, I'm in her Advanced Interpretative Arts."
Dee Dee was already at the butcher block counter
working over a head of romaine lettuce with a
vengeance. "I took her Intro to Performance Art class
my first semester. Everyone thinks she's some hippie
flake freak because of her crazy hair. ... and, okay, that
thing on stage with the yams. But she's really a nice
person. She cares about her students. And she's very
professional. She wouldn't just disappear."

"Wow," Eliza said, realizing Dee Dee wasn't just
another spooked Quimby student. For her, this was
personal.

"Yeah, right? Two of my profs are missing. God, if
my mother wasn't my mother she'd probably call the
police and have me arrested." Dee Dee sucked her
cheeks in and out, darted her eyes helter-skelter like a
villain in an old screwball comedy movie. "Hell, she
might anyway."

Eliza laughed, went by Dee Dee's side at the
counter. "Hey, how much does it owe you?" Eliza
grabbed the poor lettuce head Dee Dee was still giving
the gangster treatment.

Dee Dee dropped the knife, wiped her hands on her
apron.

"I'm sorry. And I am concerned," Eliza said. "But
let's not get carried away." Eliza hoped her young
assistant would find comfort in the very words Tom had
used hours earlier to console her. They had worked on
Eliza. *Sort of.* But now she was nursing pangs of
intuition. *There's a connection. Between all of it. But
what is it?*

"Busy in the kitchen," Eliza heard Sam say.

"Oh, well, hit me with clam chowder. And then
maybe she'll come out of hiding." Midge, who else? "If
you have any left. Oh, God, please don't tell me you're
out."

"I'll check," Sam said, as he swung into the kitchen. "Any clam chowder left?"

"I think you forgot the *stat*," Dee Dee said as she doled out what was left in the vat. "Just enough."

"That's okay; I'll do the honors," Eliza said, as Dee Dee gingerly transferred the coveted bowl to Eliza's cautious hands.

"My lucky day," Midge said, as Eliza deposited the pottage on her Greer Garson placemat.

"You bet. Just made the cut." Eliza noticed Midge was beyond happy. She was actually beaming. "What gives?"

"What do you mean?" Midge slurped the chowder. "Delish. Dregs are best."

"Dregs?"

"It's a compliment. Jeez. It's best when it sits." Midge, eyeing Eliza, shook her head. "Everyone knows that. Hey, what's with you? You look like you were hit by a Mack truck and I was doing the driving."

"Welcome to Understatement City. I'm Eliza Gordon. I'll be your guide."

"So? Details, please." Midge fondled a package of oyster crackers.

"You first."

"Well... I thought you'd never ask." Midge took in another hearty spoonful. "So good. I was jonesing through my whole show. Almost played an old Campbell's soup commercial just for the heck of it."

"Okay, so I'm asking, what's going on?"

"Oh, that. Right. Well I solved the mystery."

"Which one? The Deb Attwater murder? The disappearances of Jonas or Yolo Steinberg? Or my tweeter?"

Midge's face went slack, but just for a second. "None of the above. But I know who Sage Wisdom is."

"That tabloid hack on the *Grapevine*?"

"Yep. Wanna take a guess?"

"Not really." Eliza wasn't in the mood for trivial shenanigans. But she played along, "Okay. Lois Danziger?"

"Ah, wouldn't that be delicious?" Midge took a sip from her Diet Pepsi bottle. "But just as precious....drum roll, please! Ladies and gentlemen... Ms. Sadie Weber!"

"Are you kidding?" Eliza perked up at the revelation that WSHP's longtime receptionist and a lifelong thorn in Midge's side was the town's latest gossip monger. She also realized that that meant that Sadie must be Sweet Lorraine Dresser's best friend—the yenta who plied the eccentric detective with daiquiris so she'd spill Nathaniel Miller's name way back when the Attwater murder investigation was in its nascency. "How do you know?"

"Caught her red-handed." Midge coughed. "Well, more like red-throated. I swung by the station last night and spied her car—that old white Cadillac heap— parked across the street. So I knew something wasn't kosher. I mean, why not park in the station's lot? She was obviously trying to pretend she wasn't there."

"So why did she park so close? Or better yet, why not walk to the station? I mean she lives a few blocks away, right?"

"Right." Midge rolled her eyes, clucked her teeth. "Come on. You know who we're dealing with here. She's too stupid to realize she's not that clever with her covert parking operation. And as for the walking business—she's bone lazy."

"So what exactly did you catch her doing?"

"I nabbed her in the production studio recording her dopey podcast."

"Really? Fascinating." Eliza smiled. She was actually intrigued by all of this, though she was still distracted by all the ominous thoughts floating in her head. "But I thought Sage Wisdom had a weird, almost British accent."

"Yeah. It always sounded phony to me. It also sounded kind of muffled, the way a lot of low budget podcasts do."

"Oh, here we go. Again!" Eliza let out an exasperated sigh as she flashed her phone in Midge's face.

A new tweet from @EapsLament glared back:

@SoupOpera Ready to meet ur fate face-2-face? #justice will be served #evermore.

"Oh, God," Midge said. "You poor kid. No wonder you look so spent."

"It's all so…" Eliza bristled, then brightened as an inspired notion crossed her mind. "Hey, maybe we can use Sadie….. I mean *Sage*… for our sting operation."

"We have a sting operation?" Midge's glistening eyes said she was in.

"We might," Eliza said. "We just might."

CHAPTER 28

Things went from weird to worse.

Eliza called Isabelle, the Pixie Pastry Patrol gal with whom she had the most contact. A strange woman with an odd, piercing voice answered.

"Gone fishing. Out of business." The woman hung up.

Eliza rang back and the woman, who already sounded irritated by the inquiry, muttered: "I told you; she's run off. That's all I know."

"Do you mind telling me who you are?"

"Her sister," the woman hissed.

"Oh… and you're not worried?"

"No. She does this all the time."

"Really?" While she hadn't known Isabelle very well or for very long, the young woman had always seemed so buttoned-up and efficient. Eliza couldn't picture her as the type to just abandon her life for one of adventure on the road.

"She gets bored easily."

"And she left her phone behind?"

"That's what she does. Totally disconnects from the world. She read *Siddhartha* when she was fourteen."

"Do you know her friend… partner, Eleanor? I don't know her last name. Maybe I could get her phone number."

"Never heard of her."

The abrupt dial tone set Eliza back on her heels.

Midge—and her psychic radio waves—launched into the Doors' "People Are Strange."

Indeed, Eliza thought. And they were about to get stranger.

Eliza had already given Midge the go-ahead to plant those gossip seeds in Sadie Weber's devious little head. Within minutes, this item popped up on *The Goodship Grapevine:*

Sage Wisdom asks:
What local notable is being stalked by a mysterious and most menacing Twitter troll? We're boiling with curiosity.

Okay, so Sadie wasn't exactly Liz Smith, but Eliza figured she'd done the trick. Now all they had to do was sit back and wait for @EAPsLament to take the bait.

About an hour later the tweet arrived:

@EAPsLament @Soup Opera: Crying in public? So your style. #Justice follows. Anywhere. Anytime. #evermore.

Before she could really think it through, Eliza tweeted back:

@Soup Opera @EAPsLament OK. Let's meet. Quimby College Library. 2nd Floor computers. 3 PM Fri.

And for the rest of Tuesday and into Wednesday, Eliza waited. And fretted.

As the hours ticked by, through breakfast, lunch and a lackluster rehearsal (Colin O'Neal was M.I.A.) Eliza's soap opera imagination was in full tilt overdrive. *What the hell is going on around here?* People dropping out right and left, a menacing tweeter and, oh yeah, they hadn't really solved Deb Attwater's murder. Not to Eliza's satisfaction anyway. As she mulled the mayhem and the wheels she'd set in motion, Eliza's anxiety level rose through a frenetic Wednesday lunch. And she poured it all into a vat of Tortilla soup. One splash of Tabasco led to the next; and before long, the soup had morphed into a public swimming pool for jalapeno peppers. By the end of the day, one slurp could have kicked Adelaide La Fontaine all the way back to the Big Easy.

Tom would be furious when he learned about the sting. After all, he'd admonished her to be patient, to let the FBI handle it. She had to tell him before Friday. She had to confess. Maybe it would save their relationship. It might even save her life.

So on Thursday, after breakfast and before lunch shifted into high gear, she called Tom.

"So glad you called, honey," he said, with an urgent lilt. "I'm at Goodship Pavilion. They just brought my dad in."

"Oh, God, what happened? Is he okay?"

"Stubborn old guy. Fell off a ladder trying to prune back the apple tree." Tom sighed. "Think he broke his leg… and he may have a slight concussion."

"You want me to meet you there? I can get someone… maybe Dee Dee's friend Claire to cover."

"No, please. You know how he is. He'll be embarrassed. And they might release him soon anyway."

"Okay, I'll come by later. Send him my love."

****

Eliza stopped by the Santini house Thursday evening. Bert, his leg in a cast, all propped up on a pillow, was ensconced in his well-worn and incredibly sturdy, yet comfy, Lazy Boy. True to form he was eschewing all attempts at fussing.

"Oh, please, just a little spill," he insisted as Eliza scrawled her signature across his cast. "And he thinks *you* have a wild imagination."

"Creative," Tom called from the kitchen where he had gone to re-heat his dad's favorite clam chowder Eliza had just smuggled in from Soup Opera. "I believe *creative imagination* were my exact words. Check your sources, old man, before you take over Sage Wisdom."

Everyone was seduced by gossip, Eliza thought as she ambled into the kitchen to help Tom. *And to talk.*

But Tom wasn't as casual when she stood by his side at the stove and saw the concern in his kind eyes. "He's got to be careful. His blood pressure fluctuates. And his eyesight isn't what it used to be." Tom stirred the pot with vigor. "But you know how he is. All self-sufficient and stubborn."

"Like father, like son." Eliza offered a comforting smile as she stroked Tom's arm.

She didn't have the heart to tell him. She just couldn't. *Not here. Not tonight.*

But she couldn't call off the sting either. *In too deep.*

She sat in her car in Tom's driveway for a few minutes. *What can I do?* She checked her phone.

@EAPsLament: @ SoupOpera It's on! Tomorrow 3 PM if you dare meet #justice.

CHAPTER 29

Fifteen minutes 'til show time. And it was almost a no-go.

At two-forty-five, Friday afternoon, Eliza and Midge were standing at the Quimby College library front desk sweet talking a buzz cut in a QC security officer uniform with a serious Tums addiction into letting them in. Things had changed from those innocent halcyon days when the public could freely mill about the campus, including the hallowed halls of the pristine library. ADAM—After the Deborah Attwater murder— suspicion and caution pervaded the daily doings of campus life.

Whipping out an out-dated press pass she'd kept for such occasions, Midge swung into her media song and dance. "No, ma'am. Sorry, no can do," the officer said as bits of chalky wintergreen spewed from both sides of his crusty mouth. "Just can't be done. Not in this climate." He retrieved a new roll of antacids from the pocket of his shiny blue polyester shirt and rolled it across the desk. Back and forth, back and forth in a hypnotic ritual that somehow lulled Eliza into a temporary state of calm.

So Midge asked for Belinda Whiteside, an old Goodship High chum who was now the Quimby reference librarian. With a wink and a nod, Belinda, tapping her officious black pumps on the well maintained oaken foyer, got them in under the guise that Midge was the college's media liaison. She had, after all, updated the campus radio station a few years earlier.

"Fat lot of good it did *my* kid," Midge groused as they climbed the long staircase to the second floor computer enclave.

"Maybe we should just forget it." Eliza paced around the area in front of a long bank of cubicles, each housing either a PC or MacBook.

"Too late for that." Midge hunkered down in a center cubicle. "It's just your nerves. And anyway, did you catch that wink Belinda gave us? It comes with a heavy price tag. Believe me, you couldn't sell enough soup to pay it off."

"Sorry." Eliza exhaled a gush of anxious air. "I didn't mean to put you in a dicey position."

"That comes later. After we catch the creep, we can hit the casinos at Mohegan Sun."

Eliza scanned the area. There were sixteen people scattered about, occupying a handful of the thirty or so cubicles.

Sweet sixteen. But was @EAPsLament hiding in plain sight, masquerading as one of those college kids––ragged or preppie; hippie or neo-punk—surrounded by knapsacks and books, immersed in their work?

"How will I know who it is?"

"He'll know you," Midge said, her eagle eyes darting about the room. "What a motley crew."

"Yeah, but they look pretty normal."

Eliza shuddered as a familiar character strolled by. It was Dee Dee's friend, that taciturn guy she'd met at the Quimby gallery show. His neon green hair had been replaced by a purple Mohawk.

Him? she thought *No, not likely. But then again, why not? It could be anyone.*

The kid—his name was Dylan, she'd just remembered, and he had coal black eyes that gave off a haunted look—recognized Eliza and gave her a meek wave. That's what the hair is all about, she figured. He was trying to lighten his aura.

"A contender?" Midge whispered.

"I doubt it." Eliza sighed. "But who knows?"

Midge folded her arms akimbo, nodded with smug satisfaction.

"Check out the cubicles across from us. Serial killer, center right."

Eliza spied the kid in question: pasty grey face, squinty eyes, greasy hair and a scruffy beard; an oversized soiled white t-shirt draped over tattered jeans. "Doubtful," she said. "Too obvious. Looks like someone my mother would cast as the killer in a Lifetime movie." The kid lifted his right sleeve and as he scratched his shoulder, Eliza saw a blurry blotch, but couldn't make out the tattoo. If Margot was in charge of the production, it would be a snake. Or better yet, a skull and crossbones.

"We'll see." Midge spewed a dismissive hiss. "Real life often plays into typecasting. I mean, where do you think stereotypes come from?"

Another anxious shrug from Eliza. "Maybe," she mumbled. As the minutes ticked by, she kept checking and re-checking her phone. No love notes from @EAPsLament. Maybe he wouldn't show. Maybe that was best. Then again, maybe she'd be forever subjected to this taunting, this endless harassment.

It was already a few minutes past three when a loud, relentless buzzing reverberated throughout the quiet library. People were standing up, gathering by the landings on all four top floors as a man, his arms brimming with books scurried through the main floor. A kid shouted, "Dead man walking! Dead man walking!" And people tittered and laughed.

By now, Eliza and Midge had joined the second floor gathering. "Oh, wow," Midge blurted. "What's with that guy? Guess he likes the cooking down at the county jail better than bachelor microwaves."

Eliza realized, too, who the man was. *Nathaniel Miller*. The embattled professor, still formerly charged with Deb Attwater's murder, was here, trying, Eliza imagined, to regain some semblance of normalcy in his up-ended life. But the monitor he now wore on his ankle like a badge of culpability, signaled the authorities—and everyone else within enthusiastic earshot—that this dangerous character was roaming beyond his boundaries. Why she wondered, would he subject himself to further humiliation, not to mention probable arrest? He must have known the parameters of his home confinement when his high-profile attorney finally got him sprung on bail.

"Innocent until proven guilty!" a young woman's voice, high-pitched and nasal shouted. And then suddenly students were applauding and cheering. "Professor Miller! Professor Miller!"

Nathaniel Miller looked timorous, but somehow radiant as the books tumbled from his arms, sprawling across the library's elegant chestnut carpet. By now, he was surrounded by Quimby security officers and a few Caulfield cops who'd just arrived. As a cop slapped the handcuffs on him, Eliza noticed a big yellow splotch on Miller's blue Oxford shirt. She hoped he'd enjoyed those eggs, presumably his last breakfast as a free man, at least for a while. Then she saw a smile, sweet and grateful, enliven his weathered face. *That's why. He needed this. The adoration. The recognition from these kids. His students.*

And once again, Eliza had this gnawing feeling that he wasn't guilty. Well, not of Deb Attwater's murder anyway.

"They got it wrong," Eliza said; as she spotted Sweet Lorraine Dresser and Chief Charlie Rosencrantz join the crowded cadre of law enforcement.

"One mystery at a time, Marple," Midge jibed.

And then a vaguely familiar voice added, "So how do you account for *her* blood on his tie?"

Eliza flinched and looked up. It was Eleanor, the other half of the elusive Pixie Pastry Patrol. "Oh, hi." said Eliza.

"Sorry. Didn't mean to scare you," Eleanor said, her head hanging low. She sported that floppy Carly Simon hat she'd worn the first day Eliza had met her. "They're calling it their 'sloppy gun.'" The young woman's eyes met Eliza's now, and Eliza could see a pensive, almost troubled contortion to Eleanor' pleasant features.

"She spooks easily these days," Midge said.

"I don't know," Eliza conceded. "Oh, Midge, this is Eleanor, one of the gals who made those rum raisin doughnuts you love so much."

"Love is too casual a word. I lust after those doughnuts. I actually had a dream about them. Very sensual, let me tell you." Midge's eyes grew wide, her expression orgasmic.

"Great... thanks," Eleanor said with hesitation. "Oh, sorry about all of that."

"Did Isabelle give you any warning? I mean, she just left you in the lurch?"

Eleanor nodded. "Yeah, totally. She left me holding the bag, And I just can't keep up with the orders."

"It's so strange. I mean she just didn't seem like the type to do this kind of thing."

"You never know about people, I guess." Eleanor blanched.

"Will you continue with the business without her?" Eliza grabbed a surreptitious glance at her phone. No new tweets from @EAPsLament.

"I don't know. I'm trying to get my Master's thesis done."

"Oh, right; you're a student here." Eliza sort of knew this; she'd seen her walking through Beckett Hall once or twice.

"Perennial." Eleanor let out a disgruntled snort. "Think I'm on my last chance extension."

"What are you doing your thesis on?" Midge asked, her eyes darting around the cubicles.

"That's part of my problem." Eleanor sighed. "First I was doing it on Zelda Fitzgerald... she's underrated, you know. Then the psychopathology of Edgar Allan Poe. But now, I think I may whip something up about Raymond Carver. He's been on the shelf for a while. So to speak."

"Guess it's hard to decide. There are so many fascinating subjects to explore." Eliza was working her phone with quick trigger panic fingers.

"Yeah, guess I have a commitment problem. But I am sorry we screwed up your biz."

"We'll manage." Eliza scanned the room. It was pushing three-twenty and the menace had yet to emerge.

"Easy for you to say," Midge offered through grief-gritted teeth.

"I'm sure Michelle Dexter will be happy to pinch hit." Maybe he was waiting for Eleanor to leave; for Eliza to clear the decks. "Well, keep in touch. Let me know if you want to continue."

"Oh, okay," Eleanor said. As she readjusted her bulky drab green knapsack across her shoulder, her hat flew off. As she retrieved it for her, Eliza was stunned by the young woman's hair; it appeared newly shorn into a very severe cut that accentuated the eerie, almost desperate look in her dark eyes.

"Oops… sorry… thanks." Eleanor grabbed the hat and scampered off.

"Another one. So many odd lots," Midge said "But she sure knows her way around a doughnut."

"That she does." Eliza checked her phone again. "Okay, so where are you?"

"Maybe he was spooked by all the buzzing… not to mention cops swarming the place." Midge sighed. "Some criminals get skittish… right, Dr. Fraud?"

"Maybe." Eliza was too anxious to be perturbed by Midge's mocking.

"Oh, wait," Midge scrunched down and picked up a laminated card. "Oh, dang; she left already." It was an ID card with Eleanor's name on it. Midge handed it to Eliza.

"Eleanor Blyth-Blanchard, English Department Teaching Assistant. 2013-14. She wasn't kidding. She has been plugging away at that thesis for a long time. Well, it's expired, so she probably doesn't need it anyway."

"Wait," Midge blurted, squinting as she spied a young woman, whom she thought was Eleanor at the bank of cubicles across the way. "Oh, maybe not."

"Try putting your glasses on,"

"Why? Takes all the fun out of the guessing game." Midge laughed. "Comes in handy too, if you want to avoid someone. Just pretend you're blind as a bat."

"Blyth-Blanchard?" Eliza stared at the ID card. That name sounded familiar, but Eliza didn't know why; she couldn't quite place it.

Eliza's phone pinged and it jolted her out of her chair.

"Easy," Midge said, grabbing her friend's denim ensconced arm. They both glared at the @SoupOpera Twitter notification page:

And there it was:

@EAPsLament @SoupOpera Chickened out? I was here. Where were you? #Justice delayed, won't be #Justice denied.

"What? I was here! I *am* here!" Eliza exclaimed, but in a muted library blurt.

"So *you* are."

Eliza heard *that* voice and knew there was trouble ahead. *Big trouble.*

CHAPTER 30

The jig was up. Dee Dee had turned Eliza in.

"I'm sorry. But I was so worried," Dee Dee said, a splotch of pink crawling across her face as she loaded the take-out sandwiches into the cooler. "I saw that Twitter exchange and, well, I ... I just had to tell him."

"That's okay," Eliza said, as she and Midge slid into a back booth. It was already past four and no one else was in the eatery.

Tom followed, but remained standing, hovering over the booth, bobbing back and forth in his big black police shoes. "You're just lucky that creep never showed," Tom said, his face contorted with anger and anxiety.

"I know," Eliza said, clinging to the scintilla of concern she gleaned from Tom's kind eyes. She was lucky; she knew that, but she wasn't at the same time; because now God only knew what that menace would do. She just wanted this drama over. She wanted to solve at least one mystery. "I just thought..."

"*We* thought," Midge interjected, patting her friend's shaky hand.

Tom, holding his hand up like a traffic cop, brought the impending excuses to a screeching halt. "If any thought went into this, you would have called the whole scheme off." He was mad, really mad, Eliza knew by the way he pursed his lips together; she could practically see the cartoon smoke gush from his ears and off the top of his head.

"I almost did." Eliza hung her head, reflexively swatted imaginary crumbs off the immaculate booth table. "But it was too late. I sent that tweet and ... I just had to go through with it."

"Unreal," Tom muttered. "Then you should have at least clued me in."

"I... I know," she said. Eliza didn't want to go into the business with Bert. She didn't want to manipulate Tom's emotions, even if it was the truth. He had the right to nurse his fury.

"For what it's worth, we set the sting up in a very public place. I mean, come on, really, how much danger could we have really been in?" Midge offered.

Not exactly helping, Eliza thought as her eyes locked with Tom's.

"The *sting?*" Tom threw up his hands. "You two are too much. You really think you're starring in some late show caper."

"More like a matinée," Midge said.

Eliza cradled her head in her hands. Tom finally slipped into the booth, sitting next to Midge. *And glaring at Eliza.* "So can I at least get some soup?"

"Sure," Eliza said, as she quickly slid out of her side of the booth. "Chowder? Bisque?"

"Surprise me," Tom said, a sliver of a smile crossing his face. "Why stop now?"

"Oh, so it shouldn't be a total loss!" Midge yelled after Eliza as she headed glumly towards the kitchen.

"Okay," Eliza said as she swung into the kitchen. She wondered just how long Tom would make her squirm. Not that she didn't deserve it, but the sleuthing fiasco had all been for naught.

Or maybe not, she thought, swinging into the kitchen. Dee Dee was clunking around, trying to act busy and avoid eye contact with Eliza.

"I was just trying to have your back." Dee Dee was stowing leftover containers of smoky pea and five bean vegetable into the fridge. "I hope I didn't make trouble for you."

"It's okay. I have no one to blame but myself. Anyway, it'll pass." Eliza handed half-filled tubs of corn salad and coleslaw to Dee Dee. "How well do you know your friend Dylan?"

Dee Dee closed the large workhorse refrigerator. She stretched her young, agile body, hands over her head, striking a pose evocative of a girl from an old 1950's exercise TV show. "I don't know. Pretty well, I guess. Why?"

"No reason, really. I just saw him at the library today." Eliza doled out bowls of lobster bisque for Tom and Midge.

"Wait... you think Dylan is our tweeting menace?"

Eliza smiled. She was actually touched that Dee Dee had called the creep *our* menace. She knew Dee Dee really did have her back; she'd become so invested in Soup Opera and Eliza's well-being. "No, of course not. ... Well, who knows? But he's your friend and he did wave at me."

"I guess he's a little weird. Kinda of a loner, but he's in the artsy group," Dee Dee said, moving her head side to side. "Guess that's not a ringing endorsement. But he's pretty young. I mean, when was that soap on anyway?"

"About seven, almost eight, years ago," Eliza said with a nod. "I see your point."

"I mean he's a senior now, so yeah, maybe he could have watched it when he was in high school or junior high. But what time was it on? He was probably in school."

"I think it aired at 1 p.m. on the east coast. So you're right; he was probably in school."

"Unless he got mono or something. That's how Claire got hooked on *The Young and the Restless.* I can check if he ever got sick and spent weeks at home if you want."

"No, that's okay."

"It's mostly a girl thing anyway, isn't it?" Dee Dee took one of the bowls and followed Eliza back into the dining room. "Watching soaps, I mean. But maybe not. I shouldn't be so sexist, I guess."

Eliza nodded as they made their way back to the booth. *Mostly a girl thing? Maybe the tweeter was a girl.* "You're probably right."

Dee Dee deposited the bowl of bisque in front of Midge; Eliza delivered Tom's soup. "Just made it." She smiled.

"Delicious!" Midge beamed and started in.

"This should help." Tom tried to conceal his smile, but Eliza figured if she wasn't yet in the clear, she was at least making her way to dry land.

"What, no Oysterettes?" Midge smiled holding out an open hand.

"Oh, sorry." Eliza scampered back to the counter. "Just a little off my game today." Dee Dee was now sitting there, hunched over a book. As she grabbed a few packets of crackers, Eliza recognized the book: *Hothouse Child.* It was that book they'd been talking about a week or so ago, about a pair of shrinks and the psychological experiments they performed on their own daughter.

"What are they subjecting her to now?"

Dee Dee looked up. "Oh, get this: they took her to a maze after dark and left her there all night. She finally found her way out in the morning. Over eight hours. And she'd just turned seven. They claim, 'The experience instilled in Orchid a sense of fearless independence.'"

"Crazy."

Dee Dee earmarked her page and shut the book. Eliza noticed the cover. *Hothouse Child* by Dr. Stanley Blanchard, M.D. and Dr. Margaret Blanchard, Ph.D.

Blanchard? So that's where she'd seen that name. It can't be. Or can it?

"I'm telling you that girl… God, she's probably close to thirty by now… she's got to be a mess." Dee Dee said.

"Maybe a deadly mess."

CHAPTER 31

"I'm just saying, be very sure before you blow my chance of ever again caressing one of those doughnuts." Midge's eyes were wild and she was gesticulating like an underdog political candidate scoring points at an overcrowded debate.

With nary a late day customer, they were still gathered at that back booth—Eliza, Midge, Tom and now Dee Dee, too, listening as Eliza laid out her case against Eleanor, the half of the Pixie Pastry Patrol still hanging in town. *Lurking* might be a more apropos description of Eleanor's comings and goings. That is, if Eliza's theory about the odd young woman being the tweeter who'd been harassing her for two weeks now was on the money. And it was—she had to admit—a circumstantial case, and a flimsy one at that. Basically, it came down to a last name and a hunch. So Eleanor had the same last name as the kooks who wrote *Hothouse Child,* that crazy book Dee Dee was reading. So what? Surely *Blanchard* wasn't that unusual a name. And even if she had been the girl they'd called *Orchid* all grown up, that didn't mean she'd turned out with all her screws scrambled. But Eleanor had popped up at the library just in time for the arranged menacing tweeter meeting then disappeared only minutes before another tweet appeared accusing Eliza of not showing for the confrontation with the elusive @EAPsLament. That was something, wasn't it? *Surely something more than mere coincidence.*

"Wouldn't hold up in court," Tom said, an intent expression affixed to his face. "But it's someone to look at." Tom may have been reluctant to acknowledge it, but he'd come to respect Eliza's instincts.

"But why?" Eliza sucked in her cheeks.

"One of your *fans*," Tom said, working the air quotes.

"Some fan," Eliza said. The image of that strange woman shouting at her, calling out Bailey Barnes, the name of her *Day to Day* character at SitCom Con flashed through her mind. Could that have been Eleanor? When they'd first met, Eliza had thought the girl looked vaguely familiar. Some of these people, these so-called *fans*, become obsessed. That's what Gwen had told Eliza. Gwen's crazed fan had assaulted her with a bag of onions in the grocery store. At least, that incident had proven the catalyst to Gwen's daytime Emmy. Eliza didn't have anything to show for all her worry and sleepless nights. Of course, she didn't have a shiner either. *Always a trade-off, always a silver lining?*

"Face it: fame has its price." Midge smiled.

"Go tell that to Julia Roberts. Or the Kardashians." Eliza flicked a straw wrapper at Midge.

"In the same breath... really?" Midge clucked her tongue. "That's like eating lobster with Milk Duds. They're both delicious, but they just don't go together."

"So what's with that Twitter moniker? I mean what does @EAPsLament stand for?" Dee Dee asked.

Eliza shrugged and Midge sighed. "Wait, what did she say she was doing her thesis on?" Eliza asked, nudging Midge on the sleeve of her billowy lavender blouse.

"Oh, jeez..." Midge was working her crowded memory bank. As she rolled her eyes and cheeks around, Eliza could see the Post-it-Notes flying through her pal's head. "Damn... there were a few, I think. She couldn't make up her mind. Raymond Carver was one, I think."

"Right. Didn't she say he'd been left on the shelf for years or something?"

"He's actually making a comeback," Dee Dee said to surprised glances. "Sort of. I mean in *Birdman,* they put on a Broadway show based on his work. Michael Keaton almost won the Oscar."

"And Zelda Fitzgerald, right? F. Scott's wife," Midge said.

"Underrated, she said, right?" Eliza added.

"Talk about crazy. Didn't she spend time in the loony bin?" Dee Dee chimed in.

Tom looked askance at the eager young woman. "I think it's safer to call it a psychiatric hospital in mixed company."

"Oh, sorry," Dee Dee said with a pretend pout. "I didn't realize your were the Chief of the PC Police."

"Wait didn't she also mention Edgar Allan Poe?" Eliza's sleuth wheels were turning fast and furiously. *In directions she wasn't ready to reveal quite yet.*

"There's your EAP," Tom said.

"Ah, yes," Midge said, discreetly swiping an unopened packet of crackers from Tom's Edward G. Robinson placemat. Tom shot her a disdainful look. "If you haven't plunged in yet, the statute of limitations must have run out." .

"Poe! Talk about a whacko," Dee Dee said, biting her tongue. She tapped Tom on the shoulder. "I mean a tortured artist who battled his share of deep dish psychological demons."

"Well, that explains the *evermore, nevermore* nonsense, I guess," Midge said. "For an English grad student, her lit references are pretty sloppy."

"And scattered. Guess that might be symptomatic of her illness," Eliza offered.

"Oh here we go, Dr. Fraud," Midge sighed. She rarely squelched her irritation with Eliza's penchant for analyzing the motivations and emotional obstacles of the criminals they both enjoyed investigating.

"What's with you?" Eliza was in no mood for Midge's mood swings.

"Nothing. Just we better tread lightly."

"You two aren't treading any way... anywhere," Tom scolded.

"Yes, sir." Eliza wasn't in the mood for Tom's fatherly tone mode either.

Tom scooted out of the booth bench, punched in a number on his cell. "Agent Byrnes? Hi, Tom Santini, Goodship Police... Yes? Oh, good. I thought so. Anyway, about that other matter: we have a name to look into. Need an address and phone number for Eleanor Blanchard. May use a middle name...or is it hyphenated? Blyth... Eleanor Blyth Blanchard. Somewhere in or around Goodship or Caulfield, New York.... Great, thanks."

"Look at this," Eliza nodded, beaming at *her* guy. "And it's not even his jurisdiction."

"How about that?" Midge and Dee Dee smiled.

Tom slid back into the booth. "Anything you're involved in, anywhere you go is my jurisdiction, lady." He smiled sweetly at Eliza, falling into her majestic green eyes.

"I hate to break up this love scene," Midge said, clearing her throat. "But do you think we should get Sadie to plant another item in Sage Wisdom?"

"I don't know," Eliza arched her brow.

"Wait! Sadie, that woman who works the front desk at WSHP is Sage Wisdom?" Dee Dee shook her head. "Guess old people will do all sorts of things to amuse themselves."

"Old people?" Eliza and Midge laughed.

"You know what I mean." Dee Dee blushed a bit. "Take my mother; her new thing is matchmaking. She really wants to get Adelaide back with her husband Curious Georgie whatever."

"We'd second that emotion," Midge said, giving Eliza's wrist a little tap.

"That was before they took off for Washington in the middle of the night. I hope they come back soon or she'll start poking around my life again." Dee Dee sighed.

"Washington? As in D. C?" Eliza's wheels were spinning again.

"Yeah, a few days ago."

"Later," Tom mouthed, hung his head. "We'll talk about it later."

"You can count on that." *Who's zooming who now, Tommy?*

Eliza's phone pinged and everyone flinched.

"Uh oh," Dee Dee said.

Eliza glanced at the phone. There it was. A new tweet. Staring at her, taunting her.

@EAPsLament @SoupOpera Think you know, Bailey Barnes? Half a story is no story. #Justice #evermore? Or #nevermore? U find me 2 find out. If u dare.

"What kind of game is this chick playing?" Midge shifted in her seat.

"She obviously wants to be caught."

"But we were there!" Eliza was frustrated. "We were at the damn library."

"Chickened out, I guess," Dee Dee said.

"*If* it's her," Tom added. "I mean, we don't know for sure."

"Well, whoever it is, wants to be caught," Eliza snarled, glared at Tom. "And *she* wants me to catch her."

CHAPTER 32

"In case you hadn't noticed, it's later now." Eliza was driving Tom home.

Tom let out a weary sigh, shifted in his seat. "You gonna hold onto *his* Jeep forever? He fiddled with the radio, finally settling on WSHP.

Eliza tapped the steering wheel along with radio's peppy oldie. She knew Tom's awkward segue was spurred by both his reluctance to explain his clandestine FBI meeting on behalf of Adelaide and Curious Georgie La Fontaine and this ride in Eddie's car. She'd never thought about Tom's feeling about it; she'd never figured it as a threat to Tom or her relationship with him. For one thing she rarely drove him anywhere. And for another, she just didn't think about it. At first, she hung on to the Jeep as a sort of vehicular security blanket, a way to cling to her connection to Eddie. Though his scent—that distinct blend of Irish Spring, peppermint Lifesavers and earth—had all but faded, she could still feel Eddie's presence. She wondered now if Tom could feel him, too, and what sort of conflict that sparked. He'd been, after all, Eddie's best friend. Maybe he'd find it comforting, too. But most likely it was strange, maybe even disconcerting for him.

"Dunno. You gonna get a deputy to drive your car home every time you want to check up on me?" Tom had done just that: had one of his Barney Fifes drive his Miata back home while another gave him a ride over to the Quimby College library in a Goodship Police cruiser.

After a commercial break, the evening DJ, Johnny B. Goode, quipped, "You Can't Hurry Love. But you can give it a nudge in the right direction," as he launched into the Supremes' hit.

"That's for sure," Eliza muttered under her breath. She tapped again on the steering wheel as they stopped at a light just a few streets away from Tom's house. "Still later."

"Okay, so I didn't tell you the whole truth." Tom sighed and this one held the weight of the world in its grasp. "You were so upset about this whole tweeting business and—I don't know—I just didn't want to resurrect this crazy foolishness with Adelaide. If that makes any sense."

"I guess it might," Eliza said with a wistful smile, as she stopped at another light, this time pulling behind a shiny green Prius with a Quimby College sticker affixed to its back windshield. She, had, after all, concealed the 'sting operation' from Tom for similar reasons. "So what's the story?"

"That damn black book." He stretched his legs on the well-worn black car carpet. "I guess it's filled with some important names. At least one Senator, a few Congressmen, some Louisiana and Mississippi mucky mucks, a cable TV honcho and a few Silicon Valley tech stars."

"So what? She figured she could get big bucks for it?"

"From Georgie, yeah… in the divorce. But the feds were tipped off by an anonymous source that Bonnie and Clyde were out to blackmail the biggest names in the book."

Eliza was looking at Tom now, falling all over again for his sweet sense of decency. She missed the light changing, and an impatient chorus of car horns catapulted her into action. A black Saab zoomed by as its driver, a middle-aged woman, offered an animated gesture.

"Sorry!" Eliza shrieked as she finally turned up the long road leading to Tom's street.

"I didn't know Midge got a Saab," Tom said.

"I still don't get why you were summoned to this big confab in D.C., Doodle."

Tom grimaced; that *Doodle* got him right in the gut. "She asked me to go with them."

"Then how could you possibly refuse?"

"Well, *begged* would be a more apt description. Their lawyer … this Avery guy was overseas… London, I think, and couldn't get a flight in time."

Eliza wasn't really angry or even hurt. Tom couldn't help himself. He was chivalrous, and loyal to a fault. But she now felt solid and secure in his love and commitment to her. These past few tumultuous weeks had, in a weird way, cemented that connection.

"I just wanted to get the ball rolling on her exodus. But I should have told you." Tom looked at Eliza with an adoring glint as she pulled into the curvy driveway of the old Santini home.

"Yeah," Eliza said, smiling. "And I should have told you about our little covert *operation*."

"That goes without saying." Tom stiffened. He hated her sleuth antics. She knew that. But he'd have to get used to them. And he knew that, too.

"I wanted to. I really did," Eliza said, now gazing at Tom with sorrow and empathy. "I almost did. But then Bert got hurt and you were so worried. And… well, like Midge said, it was in broad daylight in a very public place." Eliza stopped in front of the garage and put the Jeep in park.

Tom's eyes met Eliza's. He put his arm on her shoulder. "Okay, I guess I can see that. But please… don't press your luck."

"I know. You're right," she said, leaning over to kiss Tom on the cheek.

"I mean it," Tom admonished in that fatherly tone that bristled Eliza. Then he cupped her head tenderly in his hands, caressed her cheek and kissed her with an urgency, a passion that seemed to surprise them both. "You mean too much to me. Don't ever forget that." Tom opened the passenger door.

"I know," Eliza said, still sweetly stunned. "And you, me. Send my love to Bert."

"Will do." Tom smiled as he headed to the door.

"Call me later."

"Of course," Tom said. "Or maybe I'll come over."

"Even better."

CHAPTER 33

Eleanor Blyth Blanchard didn't exist. Of course, she wasn't a mirage. But Tom had just called Eliza with the report from Agent Byrnes. "No record of any such person on any database they can find. Guess she's a figment of someone's imagination."

Some figment; some imagination, Eliza thought as she luxuriated in her oversized sunken tub. It was the amenity that all but sealed the deal for her buying her townhouse at 18 Briar Ridge. The fragrant, buoyant bubbles of lavender and chamomile usually washed away the day's woes. But today had been a perilous slog. She was okay with the Adelaide La Fontaine saga, assumed it would soon come to a happy and long distance end. But this business with Eleanor was now ever more vexing. So she was running around with a phony name. *So what? And Why?* Eliza figured the fake name was merely the tip of the unhinged young woman's crazy iceberg.

The tweeting was odd and menacing. And Eliza was now thoroughly convinced Eleanor, or whatever her real name was, had been her cyber stalker. Just how menacing the gal was, Eliza wasn't sure. But she figured Eleanor was involved with Nathaniel Miller, and maybe even the Deb Attwater murder. But the how and why remained elusive.

Eliza rushed through her post-bath routine. She hastily toweled off, letting her big light blue terry robe work overtime absorbing the sloppy wet residue. She quickly dialed Dee Dee, hoping the girl could find

Eleanor's number in the Quimby directory. She was, after all, using that erroneous moniker in her guise as a grad student.

"Uh uh," Dee Dee grunted as she perused the directory. "They only list undergrad students." Eliza could hear rustling as Dee Dee thumbed through the guide. "Oh, and faculty."

"Really?" Eliza brightened. "Including teaching assistants?"

"Yeah." More rustling. "But there's no Eleanor Blanchard or Blyth-Blanchard listed."

"Guess she lost that job," Eliza said. That laminated ID badge—over two years old now—passed through her mind. The woman herself pretty much said her time to finally finish that Master's degree was running out fast.

"Wait… you think she was Professor Miller's TA, the one who went whacko last year?"

"Maybe. I don't know." But Eliza was pretty sure. That volatile scene between the embattled prof and a crazed Eleanor at the Last Ditch Deli shortly after Deb Attwater's murder and a few days before Miller's arrest, played out in Eliza's head with such specificity she could almost smell the pastrami and pickles.

Dee Dee gasped. "Wait, you don't think she kil…"

"No!" Eliza was thinking exactly that, but she wanted to quash Dee Dee's suspicions. She didn't have any solid proof—just the creaky lurch of her sleuth wheels. "I don't know, but let's not get ahead of ourselves."

"Easier said than done," Dee Dee sighed.

"I know, but try," she channeled Tom in her attempt to curtail Dee Dee's imagination and assuage the girl's fears.

Back in the bedroom, Eliza dialed information and came up empty again; Eleanor was living her invented identity in a shroud of secrecy.

Eliza flicked on the television. One of the cable stations was running *Presumed Innocent.* That movie had been her inspired reference point back in the early days of the Deb Attwater investigation, back when she was so sure Nathaniel Miller's estranged wife Cynthia had been the culprit. But what if it had been Eleanor— the discarded teaching assistant and maybe scorned lover—who'd planted the so-called *sloppy gun*, Miller's tie stained with Deb Attwater's blood? But how could Eleanor have accessed his apartment to plant the incriminating evidence?

Eliza plopped on her mammoth bed, stroked a dozing Hitchcock and fell back against a stack of pillows. "Damn!" she said aloud, realizing she'd left her comb on the dresser. "Forget it." She was too tired to bother with the comb out, already mentally prepping for regrets as her hair was easy to tangle. Hitch was shooting imploring glowing hazel-eyed glances in her direction. She smiled weakly. Dinnertime, even past. But her feline friend would have to wait a bit longer.

On the TV, Harrison Ford, playing the unfaithful prosecutor exonerated in his former mistress's murder, had just discovered the bloody hammer his wife had hidden in the toolbox stashed for months in the basement. He knew. Without question he knew what she'd done. And why.

Chilling. Every time. Eliza had seen the movie many times and that scene, that moment of deadly recognition, hit her hard every time.

The doorbell rang and Eliza was jolted briefly out of her anxious trance. "Use your key, Tommy," she said, knowing Hitchcock was the only one who could hear her.

Another ring. The credits rolled. And another ring. And a third. "Oh, Jeez!" she called. "Tommy!"

A staccato ring-a-ring-a–ring. "Okay, Okay," Eliza said with exasperation as she lumbered out of bed, slightly groggy and moving as slow as she could and still inch her way out of the room.

"Okay! Okay!" She bolted down the short staircase.

"Forgot your key?"

"Did you give me one?"

It wasn't Tom's voice asking the question. And when she opened the door and saw who was standing there, Eliza nearly fainted.

CHAPTER 34

"Oh, my God! It's you." Eliza reflexively pummeled Jonas on his cavernous chest, encased in a loose-fitting layer of red, black and gold flannel. She stopped herself, took in the battered visage of her prodigal brother-in-law. His eyes were swollen, with a black and blue tinge shading his bruised cheeks. She hugged him and was alarmed at his fragility. She could feel his ribcage and that set off her maternal instincts. Eliza pulled Jonas in, gently now, luring him without conversation into the living room.

Then as Jonas, with a listless surrender, plopped into her sunken sofa, she blurted: "What the hell happened to you?" Jonas threw up his hands, slumped his shoulders. "You need some nourishment," she said in a tone of consolation, and without waiting for (or expecting) a response, dashed into the kitchen to fetch sandwiches and tea. Eliza fueled herself with a potent cocktail of emotions: love, anger, relief. *Guilt.* It was the guilt that stuck in her chest like a rusty knife. *Hadn't even thought about Jonas these last few days. What kind of a person am I?*

In short order she was back, placing a plate of leftover Soup Opera wraps: Cajun chicken; smoked turkey and cranberry; and grilled veggie on the coffee table. Jonas barely touched the sandwiches, nibbling ever so delicately at the edge of the veggie wrap, but he did manage to consume two shaky cups of Constant Comment tea with the herky-jerky sips of an elderly invalid.

"Why didn't you call?"

"I couldn't," Jonas said. He seemed so small, engulfed in the massive mushy mound of couch, looking so much like an infirm little boy huddled under layers of sick bed blankets. "I couldn't call."

As sympathetic as she was, Eliza needed to know what had happened. So she spent the next few minutes extracting the traumatic basics. Right before catching his plane home, Jonas had been mugged in San Francisco. He'd landed—without benefit of identification or consciousness—in the hospital. For over a week.

"They didn't know who to call," he offered, flicking his hands weakly in the air like ancient propellers. "When I came to I didn't know how to call."

Eliza's eyes squinted with incredulity. "What? You had amnesia?"

"No. But I was pretty groggy…for days. And then when I was finally with it enough, I realized didn't have my phone."

"So? The hospital wouldn't let you use their phone?"

"Yeah, but I didn't have my numbers. They were… are trapped in my phone."

Eliza shook her head. So much for technology. It was convenient and all that. But without it, people were crippled. Nobody bothered to commit numbers to memory anymore. "They still have Information." She emitted a disgusted half-laugh, half-snort. But the object of her disgust was elusive. Was it Jonas for leaving her in the lurch while he lingered alone and helpless in a far-way hospital? Or herself for relegating her concern for him to the second tier vault of her worry bank?

"I guess. But honestly I was so out of it. For days." Eliza grimaced as another pang of guilt hung on the *for days.* "I did call eventually. Tried a few times but I kept getting 'this box is full'."

"Oh?" Eliza didn't know what could have happened. She'd been checking her phone incessantly these last two weeks, not for calls but for those insidious tweets from @EAPsLament. Maybe she'd inadvertently disabled her message box. Those pangs of guilt were piling up faster than a compulsive shopper's credit card bill. So off Eliza went to the kitchen to retrieve another cup of tea. She wanted to learn what—if anything— Jonas had uncovered during his westward mission. But with his injurious condition she just didn't have the heart to press.

As it turned out, she didn't have to. That third soothing cup of spicy brew proved the charm, and Jonas spilled all with something reminiscent of vigor.

"She had a baby," Jonas said. "That was Deb's big secret."

"Whoa… when?"

"Back in Palo Alto…when she was a grad student… close to thirty years ago now." He took another quick sip of his tea. "She had a fling with a visiting professor from Cambridge."

"Wow." Eliza's sleuth wheels turned in so many directions she was actually getting dizzy. "So she didn't keep him… or *her*… the baby?"

"No, she wasn't ready. And the guy… well her friend Celia told me he wasn't exactly…"

"Marriage material?"

"Depends how you look at it," Jonas said.

"Meaning?"

"Meaning I guess he was when he married his wife back in England."

"Ouch!" Eliza bristled. "So did she even tell him about the pregnancy?"

"Celia said Deb was afraid to tell him. Apparently, he had a volatile temper. Celia said he always 'seemed off' but she wasn't sure what his story was or what exactly drew him to Deb... except he had these haunting eyes that were 'rather seductive.'"

"So she hid the pregnancy?"

"Well, some people knew. A few close friends, anyway... Celia and her husband. But she took a semester off and lived with Celia. She's the one who made all the arrangements."

"Arrangements?"

"Doctor's appointments and the adoption."

"Ah, okay." Eliza had figured as much. "Do you know who adopted the baby?"

"Yeah... friends of Celia. I met them."

"You met them?" Eliza's green eyes grew wide. "An odd couple of psychologists named Blanchard, per chance?"

Jonas glared at Eliza. "No, a nice pair of bookstore owners named Crawford."

"Oh." Eliza sighed as her sleuth wheels screeched to a disappointing halt. "Do you know if she had a boy or girl?"

"A baby girl," Jonas said.

CHAPTER 35

Tom arrived about an hour later, all smiles, ready to share a cute anecdote about one of Bert's poker buddies and an encounter with screen siren Sophia Loren. But he ditched all joyous frivolity when he found Eliza swirling around like a tornado with Toto in its eye heading to Oz.

"Look at this!" She waved her phone frantically in one hand, shook her car keys in the other. "We have to do something!"

"Calm down, honey!" Tom grabbed the phone. "Please."

But once he laid eyes on the new tweet, he understood Eliza's panic, but had no idea how to assuage it.

@EAPsLament @SoupOpera Ignoring me? At ur own peril. Others WILL get hurt! Ur choice. #Justice #evermore or #nevermore? Tick Tock!

"Okay," Tom said. As a man accustomed to confronting and often conveying bad news, he'd trained his facial muscles to comport a stoic countenance devoid of alarm. But his police chief demeanor couldn't stop the thoughts and vague strategies floating amorphously through his mind. "I understand the urgency. But I don't know what we can do."

"We have to do something!" Eliza was pacing frenetically.

"But I don't know if we can even find her," Tom said. "If it's her."

"Oh, it's *her*." Eliza was more convinced than ever. *Evermore.*

"Wait... you said she used to be a teaching assistant?" Jonas chimed in with an effervescence that seemed to have been ignited by the dangerous mystery at hand.

"Oh, hi!" Tom had been so flummoxed, he hadn't even noticed that Jonas who'd extricated himself from Eliza's mushy mound of couch was now in the high-back chair rummaging through his briefcase. "Are you okay... what happened?"

"Long story," Eliza mumbled. "Later."

"I think Kelsey... my assistant ... may know her," said Jonas. He found a Quimby directory in his briefcase. A look of panic crossed his face as he reached into his pocket. "Oh, right, forgot for a second... can I borrow a phone?"

Tom surrendered his and Jonas punched in Kelsey's number.

Jonas exchanged brief pleasantries with the woman on the other end as if he'd never gone missing. Eliza, who was filling Tom in on Jonas' traumatic excursion in the broadest strokes so she could half eavesdrop on the call and stir her own festering vat of anxious soup, wondered if Jonas had previously made contact with his teaching assistant. *Is that pesky green-eyed monster at work here? No time for that. And anyway, Jonas had tried to contact you. Your glitchy phone had blocked the messages. Too busy receiving menacing tweets from an increasingly dangerous girl.*

"Really? Oh, wow. Wait, do you mind if I put you on speaker?" Jonas fumbled with Tom's phone. "Uh, how do I do that? Can I put this on speaker?" He waved

Tom's phone in the air like a flag of surrender. "You really need to hear this."

Tom swiped his phone out of Jonas' shaky hand. He pressed the *Speaker* button. "Here ya go"

"Is it okay? Ready now?" They all heard a young woman's impatient voice coated with a scintilla of bewilderment.

"Yes, sorry... please go on. Repeat what you told me about Eleanor," Jonas said, leaning over Tom as if he'd forgotten how the whole speaker phone concept worked.

"Well, I was just saying how she lives out there in that dilapidated house... it's all the way in the woods past the nature center. I think it was her family's house. Her father died a few years ago, I think. She rents rooms now to other grad students. I went out there last year to take a look and couldn't wait to escape."

"Escape?" Tom asked. Eliza nodded knowingly.

"Well, it was creepy. The house is a dump and she had really strict rules about where you could go. It's like she had a few locked rooms. She had a big old-fashioned key ring and jangled it when she talked about her *secret spaces*. She said she was doing some important research that would change the world. That was strange, too. I mean, she was supposedly going for a Master's in English Lit. I mean, how world-changing could that be? No offense."

"None taken." Eliza chuckled. Even her stepmother, the English professor would have been amused. "Did she ever mention what sort of things she was doing behind those locked doors?"

"No, but she had this weird maze set up in the backyard. I remember thinking I don't think anyone could ever get out of there alive." The young woman paused. "A little melodramatic, I guess."

"Maybe not so much," Eliza said in a hushed tone.

"Excuse me? I didn't catch that."

Tom shot Eliza a disapproving look.

"Oh, sorry," Eliza said. "I was just wondering; do you know anyone who lives with her? Other grad students, maybe, who rented a room?"

"I think a bunch did for a while. Most couldn't take it. But I think another English grad student stuck it out. I'm pretty sure she's still lives out there."

"Do you know her name?"

"Izzie, I think. Don't know her last name. Don't think I ever did. Don't know her too well."

"Izzie? As in Isabelle?"

"Yeah, I guess"

"We have to go," Eliza said. "Now!"

CHAPTER 36

The surrender happened so fast. And without much of a fight.

Before she could really raise a ruckus, Eliza found herself riding shotgun with Tom behind the wheel of Eddie's Jeep, and Jonas in the backseat heading out to what they all hoped wasn't a house of horrors.

Tom was driving because he knew his way around the deep, deep back roads of Goodship. And with a third sleuth on the team, his two-seater Miata wasn't exactly convenient.

Eliza's plea had worked. "She's expecting me. For some reason, she's fixated on me and if I don't show up someone could get hurt," Eliza had said, imploring Tom with her well-honed passion and her captivating green eyes.

And Eliza knew Tom knew she was right. But she also knew he'd lay down the law. And so he launched into the rules, with that fatherly, police chief from on high tone that irritated Eliza: "Hang back, follow my lead. Remember, I'm the professional here." He was right, of course, she had to concede that, but reflexively she responded with ingrained teenage eye-rolls, disgusted sighs and muttered grunts.

From the backseat, Jonas offered a few more insights into Deborah Attwater's past. "Celia said her father was pretty absent. He may have died when she was a little girl."

"What do you mean *may have?*"

"Either that or he took off," Jonas added. "Celia didn't seem to know. Deb was always a little elusive, I guess. Even back then."

Secrets, Eliza thought, *are married to lies. Sometimes generations of a family can be forever damaged.*

"She was so lovely and sad back then," Jonas said, a wistful sigh caught in his voice like a ghost of an ancient kiss. "I might have even fallen in love with that woman... the young woman she was back then."

"How sad."

"Well, you know me."

"Yes, I do." Eliza thought about Jonas losing the love of his life to that cult. She feared his psyche had been so bruised he would never completely recover.

"And what am I?" Tom asked, in mock neglect. "Chopped liver?"

Eliza gently patted Tom's arm, bundled under his well-worn tan barn jacket, his protection from the chilly April night elements. "Never," she said with a smile. "You're fine... thanks to me."

"You got that right, lady." Tom beamed. "Now let me concentrate on the road. I haven't been this far out in years."

"Really? I figured the cops had to patrol every single street, even the remote ones."

"Yeah, but not the chief *cop.*" Tom punctuated the slang term with sarcastic emphasis.

"Okay, Chief. Our lips are sealed." Eliza wasn't worried about Tom. She was confident Adelaide La Fontaine had been finally exorcised from his system. And she was taking some of the credit for that. But she understood how, in small, often imperceptible ways, and sometimes in big, dramatic bolts, people are transformed with the roll of life's often unforgiving dice. She'd seen it, felt it in her own life. And though

Eliza was reluctant to admit she'd inherited—or acquired—her mother's plucky resilience. Running through four unsuccessful marriages, her mother Margot had both hardened and, in some ways, softened, over the years. That expensive union with larcenous David Lawless III had almost wiped out her fortune, and could have done her in, too. But her mom's spirit, fueled by an odd amalgam of unbridled Hollywood ambition and a giddy romantic idealism, kept her going. Margot had found salvation casting the blockbuster *Pregnant Pause*, which led to the sequel and a slew of low-rent TV producing gigs that kept her high octane stilettos in the youthful game. Eliza found herself on the cusp. She hadn't been embittered by her tenuous mediocre acting career. She'd been all but ready to surrender that to a colorful past, the makings of amusing cocktail party anecdotes, when the whirlwind of Eddie's love came her way. But since his death she'd resisted falling into the abyss of loneliness. Goodship, those precious friendships she'd forged here and her thriving little eatery had saved her from that. And her romance and now deeply entrenched love for Tom Santini caressed her heart and nurtured her soul in ways she'd feared might be forever lost to her.

Nature vs. Nurture. It was that nexus between the two that had always fascinated Eliza. The mystery at hand—or rather the mysteries—hinged on that. Or so she'd thought. But now she doubted Eleanor's connection to Deb Attwater. If the troubled young woman wasn't Deb's long lost daughter—and Jonas' revelation about the nice bookstore owners named Crawford seemed to put the kibosh on that theory— what was her motive for the murder? Had Eleanor been so scorned by Nathaniel Miller that she'd worked out an intricate plot to kill his latest lover and then frame the libidinous lothario? It didn't seem like a good motive. Then again nothing was. To go to such deadly extremes a person had to be deeply disturbed, if not legally insane. And Eleanor, if she was also Eliza's menacing tweeter @EAPsLament—and of that Eliza was certain—was obviously deranged

The Jeep took an aggressive dip over a pothole. "Sorry," Tom said. "I think we're closing in. 121 Old Settler's Pass. See if you see a sign or marker. And remember what we discussed."

Ah, the rules again. Eliza nodded, gritted her teeth. She peered out the window looking for signage among the bramble. With the info Jonas' assistant had relayed, Tom had made a quick call and discovered the house was titled to an E. Newcomb. Eleanor? Kelsey had said she thought Eleanor's dad had died. So maybe she lived all alone out here. Or with one of the grad student tenants who could put up with her craziness. Kelsey had said a gal named Izzie might still be there. Was Izzie Isabelle, the seemingly stable member of the Pixie Pastry Patrol who abruptly disappeared only days earlier? That odd call with Isabelle's alleged sister ran through Eliza's mind. The voice had seemed vaguely familiar, but distorted. Was it Eleanor? Had she seized Isabelle's cell phone? Had she been holding Isabelle hostage—or worse? And why?

"Oh, wow!" Jonas brightened from the back seat. "I remember this place. Used to come out here as a kid for Halloween. They had a big dog, always chased us away."

"Guess they weren't prepared for trick-or-treaters," Eliza said with a sly smile. For years she'd greeted nary a miniature masked visitor at the Gordon Family Museum. But last Halloween—her first at the new Briar Ridge townhouse—she had so much colorfully clad company she all but ran out of goodies.

"Be prepared," Tom said, "to stay put and wait for direction."

"Oh, damn!"

"I'm serious," Tom admonished.

"No, it's not…" Another ping and they all knew.

It was another tweet, a new perverse love note from @EAPslament

Eliza glared at it, letting it sink in. Then she read aloud:

@EAPsLament @Soup Opera Time is nigh. Coming sooner than later: Mixed Media Murder. Ignore me #nevermore or Blood on ur hands #evermore.

CHAPTER 37

"It's show time," Eliza said with a trepidatious lilt as they finally pulled up to 121 Old Settler's Pass. The house was the architectural love child of Hitchcock's haunted *Psycho* mansion and the dilapidated *Grey Gardens* Long island landmark.

"Remember what we discussed," Tom said. But his stern tone was eroded as they exited the Jeep and took in the well-lit spectacle. The place, as decrepit as it appeared, exuded the ostentatious lighting of a Hollywood set. Eliza almost expected to see Margot pop out from behind the decaying apple tree with a clipboard, commandeering a cadre of D-List extras as she gingerly tip-toed around the rotting fruit and dead branches, all the while cursing her new eight-hundred and fifty dollar Jimmy Choo stilettos.

But it was Eleanor, waiting, in washed out denim and a red beret, on the sagging porch, who helmed the impending extravaganza. "Ready for your close-up, Bailey Barnes?"

"I think we're gonna have to play this one by ear," Jonas said as the three ventured towards the rickety steps.

Tom nodded as he strode, all business, up the stairs. "Ms. Newcomb?"

"Okay, let's follow his lead." Eliza clutched Jonas' arm as the two hung back, loitering at the bottom of the steps, looking this way and that. Eliza thought she heard something—purring, maybe. Or whimpering, coming from behind the house. But it didn't last long and, suddenly, there was odd, discordant music emanating from inside.

"I see you brought your entourage," Eleanor said, looking through Tom and glaring at Eliza with those deep-set burnt coffee eyes. "So predictable."

Eliza tentatively lurched forward, inching near the rickety stairs. "Give Tom a chance," Jonas said, holding her back.

"Ms. Newcomb, I have a few questions." Tom moved closer, encroaching on Eleanor's comfort zone, hoping to obscure her view of Eliza.

"Do you have a warrant?" Eleanor reached her hand out, craned her neck around Tom, her hot glare hitting Eliza right between the eyes.

"Is there something you don't want us to see?"

"Not at all," Eleanor snipped. "If I was hiding I wouldn't have set out the strobes, now would I?"

"So I'll take that as an invitation to come inside." Tom inched ever closer, pushing a foot across the aged threshold. *He's good*, Eliza marveled.

"Only if she comes in first."

"Ms. Newcomb…" Tom's impatience was peeking through his stoic, no-nonsense police demeanor.

"That's okay." Eliza trotted up the steps with Jonas close behind. "That's what I'm here for."

"It'll be okay," Jonas whispered as he nodded at Tom.

"Really," Eliza said with a weak smile as she reached that top shaky step. "We're all friends here, right?"

"Not exactly," Eleanor said, following Eliza's every move with her penetrating eyes. "But you've come to play, so have at it." She moved aside and ushered Eliza through the front door, letting Tom and Jonas follow without obstruction.

Eliza smelled something familiar. And comforting. *Fresh popcorn popping.*

Stunned speechless, she took in the interior. In a stark contrast to the outer decrepitude, the foyer, at least, was pristine, evocative of a small art house movie theater lobby. There was a bar fashioned like a concession stand with a vintage popcorn machine doing its business. A tray of candy boxes were on display with hand-written cards sporting ironic outsized multiplex prices.

Eleanor bopped behind the *concession stand*, with a maniacal smile. "Want some popcorn? Or maybe a little candy?"

"No thanks." Eliza darted her eyes around the room. Framed posters of an odd array of movies hung strategically on the walls. *The Bad Seed; Losing Isaiah; Juno; Damien: The Omen II.* And *Our Very Own,* the classic 1950 film that starred Ann Blyth and had recently nursed Eliza through part of a long sleepless night. *Blyth,* she wondered. *As in Blyth-Blanchard?* What was the connection? Surely there had to be one. They had stepped into a well-decorated delusion.

"On the house, of course." Eleanor smiled. *Almost normal,* Eliza thought, trying to avert her eyes from a full-blown stare. Besides the haunting dark eyes, Eleanor had a pleasant face dotted with dainty features that betrayed her inner turmoil.

"I'll try a little," Jonas offered, channeling Midge.

Oh, God, Midge. Eliza knew Midge would absolutely flip out over this delicious set-up. The kitsch. The suspense. *The candy.* And Eliza knew she'd get an earful from her missing sleuthing partner.

As Eleanor doled out a small bag of popcorn, Eliza saw the big poster behind the counter. She held back a gasp. A blood curdling poster of the 1960 horror classic *House of Usher*, starring Vincent Price. The cult flick was based on a story of family madness by Edgar Allan Poe. Eliza knew. Of course, she already knew, but now any iota of doubt had been erased. Eleanor was @EAPsLament, her tormenting tweeter.

"So you're a big social media fan?" Eliza took a shot. Jonas sighed as he nibbled on his popcorn.

Where had Tom gone? Eliza figured he was milling about, assessing the place for weapons and hostages. She guessed he'd assumed she'd be safe with Jonas as her chaperone. And Eleanor did *seem* harmless. Or at least un-armed.

"You sure you don't want anything?" Eleanor asked, shaking a box of Junior Mints. "You look like a movie candy type of girl."

Eliza offered a dismissive wave and whispered, "No thank you."

"Suit yourself." Eleanor went about with her busy work behind the counter. *The big stall.* Eliza was familiar with the posture having adopted it for eavesdropping at Soup Opera with some regularity.

Adoption. Bingo! That's what all those movies had in common, she realized. All those films, with the possible exception of the Edgar Allan Poe adaptation—but that one was self-explanatory—had adoption as a key theme or pivotal plot point. This girl was obsessed. Whether or not she was Deborah Attwater's birth baby.

"So what's your deal with Twitter?" Eliza tried to sound casual as Jonas coughed his way through a handful of popcorn.

Eleanor's faced remained expressionless. "Seduction. Works every time." So the jig was up. And she didn't care. As she said, she'd lured Eliza here with taunts (and not so) veiled threats. *What a game. But what were the rules?* "But you know that. It's your specialty, Bailey Barnes."

"I'm Eliza Gordon. Bailey Barnes was just a character I played on a soap opera like eight years ago. For nine months."

"Nine months," Eleanor said with a scorching snarl. "A lot of things can happen in nine months."

"Yes, I guess you're right." *Wow. The troubled young woman was fixated on everything related to birth and adoption*

"Clarice was abandoned, too. Did you even know that? Do you care?"

"Clarice?"

"Come on; you remember Clarice. The woman you screwed over... back in Everest Falls. Remember? Before you faked your own death."

"Clarice was another *fictional* character on *Day to Day*. It was a soap opera. Just a TV show. None of it was real."

"Don't play me. I used to live there,"

"In Everest Falls?"

Eleanor nodded. "For three years. I watched my real life live itself out while I nursed that drooling, petulant drunk."

Ah, Eliza was getting at something. "Your mother?" *Maybe.* "You were taking care of your mother?"

Eleanor squealed. "Mother? Ha! She ditched when I was three."

"Your father?"

"That lout was never my father. Just some drunk who stumbled around the place smelling to high heaven. He yelled every damn day and threw his dirty laundry and boxes of Hamburger Helper at me from the time I was five. I was so young the first two years, I used to put the box on a plate and throw ketchup over it. Great dinner, right?"

"I'm sorry." Eliza could only imagine the other atrocities the young Eleanor had been subjected to.

"No you're not," Eleanor hissed. "For years I ate cereal straight from the box most nights. He ate his soaked with Jim Beam. And just when I was free, when I finally went off to college he gets sick and forces me back to nurse the ungrateful, stinking creep. Took the stubborn bastard six years to finally kick."

"I really am sorry." Eliza extended her hand; Eleanor flinched and rubbed her back on the wall. *Self-soothing*, Eliza guessed. "No one should have to endure that."

"Holt was my father for a while." Eleanor, her eyes closed, was rocking back and forth. "But you killed him. Right after you stole him from Clarice."

"I didn't... didn't want to. I was just reading the lines, playing a part."

There was a loud thump and they all shuddered.

A panicked pink streak flashed across Eleanor's cheeks. "Hey, where's that aging Ken Doll official police chief guy you came in with?"

Perfect timing. Tom reappeared. In the entryway. "Ms. Newcomb, you have a big house with a lot of rooms."

"So?"

"So most of them seem to be locked."

"Is that a crime all of a sudden?"

"No," Tom conceded. "But if you live alone why would you have to lock them?"

"Maybe I'm locking myself out of my own life."

"Excuse me?"

"Ask Bailey Barnes here. I'm pretty sure she understands what I'm talking about."

Eliza shook her head. "Later," she mouthed.

"Hello! Hello! Is someone else here?" A weak, disembodied female voice rattled everyone. *Where was it coming from? And who did it belong to?*

That discordant music, the sort you'd hear on the soundtrack for a horror movie, blared again. Then abruptly stopped. Eliza looked at Eleanor who was behind the counter fiddling with knobs on an old fashioned tape recorder.

"Hello? Please…. I'm upstairs."

CHAPTER 38

"No more games, Ms. Newcomb. Who else is here?" Tom was fuming as he loomed over the petite menace. "You need to take me to her right now."

Eleanor jangled a large silver key ring. "No need to get all huffy and hysterical," she hissed. "I summoned Bailey Barnes, remember?"

Eliza winced, exchanged weary glances with Jonas.

"Are you keeping someone here against her will?" Tom was in full-tilt police chief mode. And for once Eliza was grateful for it.

"Not exactly." Eleanor offered a coy wink as she flashed a sinister smirk. "Follow me." She lured the trio up a winding staircase, and seemed to jangle that key chain a little louder with every creaky step.

"Ms. Newcomb—" Tom stopped in his tracks as Eleanor opened up one room.

Eleanor guided the group in with an efficient usher's wave. "Have a look-see." Eleanor beamed her laser gaze straight at Eliza. "Look familiar?"

Eliza gasped. The room was an exact replica of Holt Sinclair's study—a main set for *Day to Day*. Eliza shuddered at the sight of the bust of Clayton Sinclair. *Oh, God*, she thought, *I—Bailey killed Holt with that bust.*

Tom paced the room, opening the closet, drawers, looking behind the handsome weathered leather couch. "Enough with the games, Ms. Newcomb. Where is this person?" He was working hard to contain his ire, but

Eliza could see a slight contortion in his face, the brief flaring of his nostrils.

And Eleanor knew she was getting to him, too. "Don't hold back, Chief. If you hold back all that anger, it'll foment into rage and you're apt to implode like Inspector Anton. You remember him, right, Bailey Barnes?"

"Who?" Eliza stood, mouth agape, mesmerized by that bust.

"In Everest Falls," Eleanor said. "You have a very convenient memory, don't you, Bailey Barnes."

"I'm not Bailey..." Eliza stopped herself. She was sucked into this girl's delusion whether she liked it or not. *Don't get her angry. Go along with the gag.* "Now I remember—Inspector Anton; he had a nervous breakdown after Holt's death."

"His death, yes," Eleanor was now standing next to Eliza, once again vigorously jangling those keys. "Some would call it a *murder*."

Eliza shook her head. "I guess it was." She couldn't conjure the courage to touch the bust, but Eleanor caught Eliza staring at the regal weapon.

"It's amazing what you can find at auctions." Eleanor fondled the bust, a deranged expression seeping into her face.

Eliza moved back to the imposing antique desk. She noticed Jonas fixated on a Quimby College snow globe. *A replica of another murder weapon? Did Eleanor get it before or after Deborah Attwater was killed? Did she do it?*

There was one book on the desk. Eliza picked it up. *Hothouse Child.* "You have a fascination with this, don't you?" Eliza waved the well-worn tome. "You call yourself Blyth-Blanchard. Why?"

"I like that movie. The one with Ann Blyth. She's adopted and they love her so much she doesn't even care she came from trash. Hell, even the trashy birth mom turned out okay in the end."

"And the Blanchard part?"

"I was Orchid for a while."

"But the Blanchards... they... well, they did all these mean, maybe even crazy things. All those experiments. They don't come off as nice people."

"So? Nice is overrated," Eleanor said. "At least they took an interest."

"Please... is someone there?" The disembodied voice again. Now it was louder. Closer. And more desperate. "I'm here! Please! Someone!"

"Ms. Newcomb! Who is that? Take us to her." Tom encircled the small deranged woman, leaving no space for escape. "Now!" Tom strode back into the hallway.

"Okay, okay," Eleanor sniffed. She stomped through the study and back into the hallway, jangling the keys with an angry authority. Eliza followed first, then Jonas.

Eleanor walked down a long corridor and opened the door to the last room on the right. "Your cavalry has arrived."

They all entered the dark room, illuminated only by the light on a large TV screen. The sound was turned down but Eliza saw *The Omen II* flickering on the screen.

Eliza spied a fragile, familiar figure sit up on a large paisley print couch.

"Oh, thank God! The weak young woman said in a breathless gush.

CHAPTER 39

Isabelle. It turned out she was Isabelle *Crawford*, the adopted daughter of those nice book store-owning California Crawfords who Jonas had met during his sleuthing mission. That meant it was Isabelle, and not Eleanor, who'd been Deborah Attwater's birth baby.

It all came out in groggy dribs and drabs. Eleanor had been drugging Isabelle, slipping valium into strawberry milkshakes for nearly a week, ever since Isabelle had confronted Eleanor after discovering @EAPsLament's menacing tweets to Eliza, along with some other strange and incriminating e-mails and text messages on her deranged pal's phone. The target of those other taunting missives? Professor Nathaniel Miller. And Deb Attwater.

"Guess snooping can kill you," Isabelle said in an ethereal voice. Tom and Jonas glared at Eliza, while she marveled at the young woman's sharp wit, intact despite her medicated condition.

Eleanor spewed a bitter chuckle. "How many drama queens does it take to screw in a light bulb... or exact justice?" She paced about the room, stealing glances out the big window. "I said I wouldn't hurt you. And I haven't. Just afforded you a little hiatus... while I took care of business."

"What sort of business is that, Ms. Newcomb?" Tom was circling, looming now over the couch, cell phone in hand.

"We all know what we're talking about," Eleanor sneered. Another glance out that window. Eliza casually inched closer. "But don't expect any Perry Mason moments. I'm not confessing... to anything." The girl's gaze engulfed Eliza again, watching her look out the window. Eliza thought she saw something, *someone,* rustling through the hedges out back. *The maze Kelsey was talking about?*

"I still can't believe this." Isabelle was struggling to sit up. "It wasn't your business. Why did you do this?"

"You wouldn't do anything," Eleanor scoffed, dashed to the window, hastily pulling stained antique white drapes closed. "Justice was at hand and had to be meted out. Don't you see that?"

"No! It wasn't yours to mete out. It has... *had* nothing to do with you."

"Did you know... about the adoption?" Eliza asked Isabelle as she helped arrange a bank of pillows behind the weak young woman's back.

"I knew I was adopted. Had since I was like four or five. They told me my mother was a nice woman who couldn't take care of a child," Isabelle said, sitting upright now. "That was enough. I never needed more. Never cared to find out. They were... *are* my parents."

"Then why did you want me to investigate?" Eleanor huffed. She spied Eliza watching Tom, talking in hushed tones on his cell phone in the corner.

"I didn't. I never wanted that. Never asked you to do anything." Isabelle shook her head. "You're the one who went snooping around my dad's study last Thanksgiving."

"You wouldn't so I had to."

"Why?"

"She abandoned *us.*" Eleanor was now perched on the couch next to Isabelle, fiddling with a bag from Max's Last Ditch Deli. "You never ate your sandwich." She pulled out a limp corned beef on rye.

"*Us?*" Isabelle shot Eleanor a look of disdain. "God, you're beyond nuts."

"We're sisters," Eleanor said, biting into the soggy sandwich. "Sometimes I *am* you."

Crazy, Eliza thought. *And murderous.*

"Ms. Newcomb, I have to advise you that you have the right to remain silent," Tom said. "May I suggest you exercise it."

Stunned, Eliza tossed an imploring look in Tom's direction. *Not a great time to go by the book, Tom.*

"It's okay; I told you I'm not confessing to anything."

It may have been her imagination, but Eliza could have sworn she heard that whimpering come from outside again. And she'd seen something or someone rustle by in that elaborate maze just moments earlier. *She definitely saw that.* "Who's that? Who's out there?" Eliza asked, working the creaky drape rod.

"Who?" Eleanor looked up. "Oh, out there? Just another guest."

"Who is it, Ms. Newcomb?" Tom checked his watch. If history was any indication, Eliza figured a swat team would be circling the place within minutes.

"That Yoyo woman."

"Yolo? Yolo Steinberg?" Eliza and Jonas stared out the window. "Why is she back there?"

"How should I know?" Eleanor was now sitting akimbo, rocking back and forth, her eyes shut. "Probably working on one of her hideous performance art pieces."

"Oh, God!" Isabelle gasped. "She's still here? You said you let her go days ago. It's got to be at least a week."

"Five days," Eleanor said. "Again with the drama."

"Did you at least give her something to eat?"

"Of course," Eleanor said, clutching the deli bag. "I feed all my guests."

"For God's sake, she's a vegetarian." Isabelle started to cry. Eliza and Jonas ran out of the room and out to rescue Yolo from the maze.

Tom whipped out his handcuffs. "Take me to her, Ms. Newcomb," he said, slapping the silver bracelets on Eleanor's thin wrists. "The game's over."

"What's everyone getting all hysterical about? She's fine." Eleanor snarled her bitter hiss. "Every sandwich comes with a pickle."

CHAPTER 40

The Thursday after last Friday's Big Reveal, events were still unfolding at a breathless clip.

"Real shocker," Miriam Sussman snipped. She swatted the back of the *Goodship Gazette* Georgia Rhodes was reading at the Soup Opera counter. "That legal vampire won't be satisfied until he sucks every last drop of tabloid blood out of that crazy girl." She tapped her glass, motioning Eliza for a third refill of her bottomless lemonade.

Eliza shook her head as she refilled coffee cups around the counter. That crone used the tangy elixir as a lubricant for her indelible scowl. But Miriam was right. After dwarfing his stained and stunned client, Nathaniel Miller, with his own four thousand dollar Armani charisma, Andrew Gregorian, cashed in on the hapless professor's innocence with brash talk about potential civil remedies for such "a flagrant rush to judgment." But the fickle cable TV attention span was already moving on. And so was Gregorian, who, in hopes of signing a new high-profile client, had shuttled back to the Westchester County jail where Eleanor Newcomb was now residing.

"Too bad she confessed," Georgia said, feeling the heat of incredulous counter glances. "I mean for her case."

Miriam sniffed, tapped her empty glass again. "She may be crazier than an outhouse rat, but she's as sly as a fox, too, that one."

Georgia's eyes widened. And as Miriam gave her the once-over, Georgia adjusted the collar of her wrinkled purple tie-dyed caftan, which she'd stumbled upon during her first spring closet clean-up in fifteen years.

"Don't be such a ninny," Miriam said, smiling when Eliza finally gave renewed life to her glass. "She's fixing to run her own insanity defense scam."

"How can it be a scam? She's obviously seriously sick."

"Naivety after fifty can be construed as stupidity," Miriam clucked. "Anyway, Gregorian's sharp; he'll have the confession tossed. Half of it was given to Tom Santini, the other to Rosencrantz and that Westchester County investigator woman." Miriam tilted her head in the direction of the side booth where Sweet Lorraine Dresser was devouring a sloppy Joe with Sadie Weber, the WSHP receptionist who was nursing a bowl of chicken noodle.

Eliza resisted the conversation as she took orders down counter from Pippa De Long and Declan Rinaldi. But she knew Miriam was onto something. By all accounts, Eleanor, who'd spilled a bottomless barrel of demented beans on Friday, had since decided to clam up. There were even rumors of a hunger strike. And with all the sordid angles and Gregorian's voracious public persona the case would surely play out its fifteen minutes and then some with both cable TV allure and Hollywood treatments. The barrage of messages from Margot gave Eliza a front row seat to the pending hoopla.

"Won't be worth the paper that damn diploma is printed on," Lois jibed as Dee Dee vigorously plopped a bowel of roasted root vegetable on her mother's Joan Crawford placemat. "And no room at *the* inn with that sort of service." The rattled hotelier dabbed napkins on her damp placemat, her eyes catching the glee in her daughter's.

"That's okay; I'd rather panhandle than listen to broken records all day." Dee Dee shuffled back into the kitchen.

"We lost Yolo Steinberg," Lois said.

Eliza delivered Lois' tall unsweetened iced tea. "She's just taking a year off."

"She's not coming back," Lois sighed. And Eliza figured she was right. After being treated for dehydration and shock for one night at Goodship Pavilion Hospital and then released, the award-winning performance artist decided to go on a medical leave for the last few weeks of the semester, followed by an "indeterminate sabbatical."

Nathaniel Miller's future was shrouded in uncertainty, too. While the shell-shocked professor meekly told reporters at a brief presser that he'd hoped to return for the fall semester, Gregorian hushed him with talk of civil litigation. And the popular prof was a no-show at a rally students had mounted on his behalf in front of the Beckett administration building Tuesday.

"It's such a shame what they put that poor man through," Georgia said, tearing up.

"Well, he has to take some of the blame," Miriam snipped.

"How do you figure?"

"Well, if he wasn't such a slob, that crazy girl wouldn't have gotten the idea to frame him with his own tie."

Eliza exchanged glances with Declan and Pippa. *Score another one for that bitter curmudgeon.* Before locking her lips, Eleanor had confessed to swiping a few of Miller's ties, all conveniently pre-stained. Then after bludgeoning Deborah Attwater to death with the now infamous Quimby College snow globe, she'd actually collected some of Deb's blood, spooned out with an antique tablespoon she'd claimed was bought at an auction of items once owned by Edgar Allen Poe. Beyond the obvious macabre connection, Eleanor's obsession with Poe seemed to be related to his own fractured family. After his parents had died when he was just a baby, he'd been raised by a loving foster mother, but had clashed, mostly over money, with the woman's husband. The deranged young woman had smeared one of the ties with Deb's blood and, with the key she had copied during her brief, volatile fling with Miller, snuck back into his messy apartment and planted the evidence in his crammed hoarder's closet.

Jonas, already back in class and armed with a brand new cellphone, was well enough to greet Isabelle's parents—the Crawfords—when they came across country to care for their daughter. He was right; they were a lovely couple. After heading home for a rest, Isabelle vowed to return to complete her Master's and re-launch the Pixie Pastry Patrol. And those kids, erroneously accepted due to that website glitch? Jonas happily reported to Eliza that they'd all been offered admission, though no one knew how many applicants would matriculate given the notorious patina the college was now covered under.

"Oh, get a load of this!" Lois flashed a wry smile. She waved her iPhone, now featuring an item of fascination making news on *The Goodship Grapevine*. "This is just too delicious!" She smacked her lips and passed the phone around to random patrons.

"Must be a menopausal mood swing," Miriam chirped.

As Lois rolled her eyes, Eliza realized it was a Danziger family trait. *Apple, tree, nurture, nature. In so many ways,* Eliza thought, that's how this case, this tragic story of Eleanor could be boiled down. *If only her own parents had loved her, nurtured her, none of this would have happened. Well, at least she'd have had a fighting chance.*

"You have to see this," Lois said, thrusting her phone into Eliza's face. "Now!"

"Okay." Eliza wiped her hands on her colorfully soiled apron. "What's the big story *now?*" She grabbed Lois' phone. *Ah, so that's it. She has a record.*

Speaking of records, Midge trudged through the melodic Soup Opera door, her entry punctuated by a chorus of titters from the counter crowd.

"You're early," Eliza said, suppressing a smile as she glanced at the lopsided clock next to the *Duck Soup* poster, noting it had yet to close in on two.

"That's the beauty of 'Light My Fire'—the album version. And an eager intern who just mastered segueing into the national news." Midge grabbed the last vacant stool—right between Lois and Miriam.

"So what'll you have?" Eliza asked.

"I'm officially not talking to you."

"Oh, so I guess I can ignore the noise emanating from your moving lips."

"I'm not talking to you," Midge said as she eyed Lois and Miriam's suspicious glances. "But I am ordering. And I have it on good authority that the 'one who got away,' finally went away. So can I take it the spicy tortilla is coming in with a low roar?"

"Yes, on both accounts." Eliza smiled. "One spicy tortilla, Dee Dee. Stat!" she called into the kitchen.

After Friday night's ordeal, Eliza was thrilled to learn that the ballad of Adelaide and Glorious Georgie La Fontaine had hit its last local note. Their attorney, the elusive Avery Cummings, had finally blown through town, and with some clever legal maneuvers managed to thwart the FBI's extortion investigation. The estranged couple had last been seen in an amorous embrace right before checking out of the Goodship Inn and fleeing town in a limo. Eliza was sure Adelaide had the notorious black book stashed in an undisclosed location for future leverage. Adelaide bid Tom farewell via a voicemail message: "Thanks for all your help, Doodle. Ta ta."

"So how was Vermont?" Eliza asked Midge as Dee Dee delivered the coveted spicy tortilla to Midge's James Cagney placemat. "Did you enjoy returning to the scene of the crime?"

"So to speak," Miriam said, a bitter snicker attached to her every word.

"What's with everybody today?" Midge scanned the counter crowd, noting incredulous glances and strange smiles. "I can't believe I go away for a few days and the whole damn thing goes down. Couldn't save a little intrigue for me?"

"Sorry," Eliza said with a sly smile. "That's how it unraveled."

"Oh, don't worry," Lois said. "You didn't miss *everything*."

Eliza tossed Midge a packet of crackers. "So did it work? Did Hannah fall in love with UVM or Bennington?"

"Yep." Midge nodded. "UVM. After all the drama, looks like she's headed to her mama's alma mater."

"Really? I'm surprised they let you within fifty miles of that campus," Miriam said.

"Why? What are you talking about?"

Lois slipped her phone over to Midge's placemat. "Here, take a look."

A hot rush of red scorched Midge's cheeks and sprinted down to her neck. "Oh, dear, lord!" she blurted out. "I'll kill her! I'll absolutely once and for all put that scarecrow out of *my* misery!"

"It wasn't me," Sadie Weber said as she slid out of her booth. "I swear."

"She wouldn't dare," Lorraine Dresser backed up her life-long friend, while still munching on a side order of onion rings.

"She's right," Eliza said. It's not in Sage Wisdom. It's…"

Midge took a closer look. "Oh, cripes. Not the cover story?"

"Afraid so."

And there it was; the headline boldly flashing across the website's home page: LOCAL RADIO STAR's ARREST RECORD & TRUE ID REVEALED

And with those crushing words, and the grainy photo beneath them, Midge's secret was finally revealed. Staring back at Midge was a mug shot from twenty plus years earlier, when as a spirited and socially conscious college student in the early '90's, she'd been arrested at an anti-Apartheid protest rally in Burlington, Vermont. Under the photo the caption read:

Mug Shot uncovered of local DJ, Midge Sumner, whose real name is *Mildred Denise Sumner.*

The story continued to explain that Midge's fingerprints had been captured on the snow globe used to bludgeon Deborah Attwater.

"What your poor father went through back then," Sadie said, sucking her tongue against her teeth's noisy plaque. "The man was beside himself. Called in all the chips he could to keep it out of the local press." She rattled her head, giving her grey mop top hair a vigorous work-out.

"What's the big scandal?" Georgia asked. "It was a good cause. Civil disobedience. Nothing to be ashamed of. If anything, that mug shot is a badge of honor."

"On the bright side, it's not such a bad photo. You look so young," Lois said.

Midge grabbed another glance, smiled. "Yeah, and look at how thin I was."

"Such a beauty. But Mildred?" Eliza could no longer contain her laughter. "So *Mildred*, why did you conceal your true identity all these years?"

"Isn't it obvious? I mean, no one named a kid Mildred after 1950."

"Well, your parents obviously did," Lois said.

"Yeah, thanks, Mom. She had to be big fan of *Mildred Pierce*."

"And I bought that story about your mother loving Tootsie rolls." Eliza sighed, flung a rag in Midge's direction. "How gullible can a girl get?"

"How do you think I got my nickname?" Midge laughed.

"Every lie contains a grain of truth," Pippa piped in.

"But I saw your driver's license," Eliza said.

"Another remnant from my misspent youth," Midge said. "Let's just say I knew my way around fake IDs."

"Another badge of honor?" Miriam snickered, threw a dagger in Georgia's direction.

"So no one ever knew?"

"Gus knows."

"We all knew," Miriam said.

"I didn't," Lois said, with a pout. "And you didn't either. Or you would have wielded it like a rotting lemon wedge."

Miriam stiffened to a chorus of counter cackles. "Be that as it may, your cluelessness doesn't exactly bode well for your future as a professional snoop sister," she jibed Eliza.

"Guess I'll have to continue to compete on the amateur circuit." Eliza smiled.

****

By the time Tom came into Soup Opera, with Bert happily hobbling along on crutches, the boisterous lunch crowd had all but petered out.

"Oh, good… reinforcements," Eliza said, as she tried to negotiate the poster of *Mildred Pierce* off the back wall. "You can find a place for this, right?"

Midge laughed as she ambled to Eliza's side. "I guess I could squeeze it into my closet of an office. I mean now that I'm out of the closet." She noticed a sparkle on Eliza's left hand. "Wait, is that?"

Eliza nodded. "Saturday night," she said, flashing the finger that boasted Tom's mother's engagement ring. "He popped the question."

"Finally," Midge said, as Tom approached.

"So glad you approve…. *Mildred.*"

"And the hits keep on coming." Midge sighed, resigned to the realization that the glow of this particular humiliation wasn't about to fade any time soon. "So did you set the date yet?"

"We don't believe in long engagements," Bert chirped from his perch at the center table.

"See what we've gotten ourselves into?" Tom lightly kissed Eliza on the cheek.

"I'm sure we can do better than that." Eliza passionately kissed Tom on lips.

"Just wait until the show wraps," Pippa chimed in, as she scrawled witty well wishes across Bert's leg cast. "Then I'll help you mount the biggest prod…wedding this town has ever seen."

Epilogue

"I've heard of opening night jitters," Tom said, lounging with Hitchcock on Eliza's enormous sleigh bed. "But closing night yips? That's a first for me."

Despite mediocre local reviews, the three-weekend run of Pippa De Long's stage version of the classic 1940's movie *The Great Lie* had garnered boffo box office returns thanks to pugnaciously persuasive word-of-mouth and Wendy Orenstein's well-worn and militant Rolodex. But at the wrap party, Eliza took one look at the burrito buffet and spent twenty excruciating minutes in the restroom followed by a round of brisk air-kisses and show biz waves before Tom escorted her home.

"Sorry," Eliza said, emerging from the bathroom, now snuggled under her oversized blue terry cloth robe. "Sorry I ruined the party for you."

Tom beckoned her over with a royal gesture. "Big sacrifice," he said. "Considering I'm always the belle of the ball." He laughed.

"And what a beautiful belle you are." Eliza smiled as she sat on the bed.

"I don't get it. I mean, I actually ate one of those monstrosities. You just gave them a passing glance."

"Think it may have been the smell."

Tom noticed Eliza's pasty complexion. "You still look a little green around the gills, honey. You okay?" He patted the purple checked blanket. "Come closer."

Eliza scooched over to Tom's side. They canoodled for a bit, serenaded by Hitchcock's imploring purrs.

"Don't even," Eliza said as she petted the perpetually ravenous cat. "Even the thought of a late night cat snack…" She grimaced.

"Still it was a great night." Tom beamed. "And you were magnificent. But I mentioned that already, right?"

"Several times." Eliza smiled, sunk her head deeper into Tom's arm fold. "But thanks. It's always nice to hear."

"I'll have to tell you more often." Tom caressed her cheek. "So what do you think about Christmas?"

"What about Christmas?" Eliza sat up.

"For the wedding." Tom smiled. "Well, maybe the week before. Or a few days later, between Christmas and New Year's. Everyone should be around. We can go all out and book the Goodship Inn."

Eliza glowed through her clammy complexion. "Look at you, all romantic. It looks good on you, Tommy." She kissed his cheek.

"I'm sure Lois would love it," Tom said.

"Pippa, too… and Bert will be over the moon," Eliza said. "But by Christmas I think we may be getting ready for another celebration." Eliza stuck her hand in her robe's mammoth pocket and pulled out a colorful EPT stick, waving it in Tom's face.

"You're kidding?" Tom's eyes widened as he bolted upright.

"Nope." Eliza smiled. "Buckle up, Tommy. Ready or not, here we go."

"Oh, I'm ready," Tom said. "We can run off to Vegas tomorrow. Tonight, if you want. I'm sure there's a twenty-four hour chapel with an Elvis impersonator waiting to croon us into happily ever after."

"Slow your roll, Chief." Eliza laughed. "I'm sure we can find a happy middle ground."

Tom took a deep breath. He fell into Eliza's alluring green eyes; they could both feel the future unfold before them like a romantic movie montage.

The cinematic reverie was pierced when Tallulah sauntered into the room, sparking a hiss-off with Hitchcock. "Kids!" they said in unison.

"But there's one thing we have to get rid of before we make it official," Tom said.

"I know." Eliza nodded. "The Jeep."

"The Jeep?" Tom shook his head. "I don't care about the Jeep. I mean, get rid of it if you want; it's getting old. Wait… now that you mention it, I guess I should trade in the Miata, too. It's not exactly practical for a growing family."

"No, I guess not," Eliza said, snuggling back into a comfortable position under Tom's arm. "So what then?"

"That sofa. Sorry, but that sofa's gotta go."

"Oh, God, yes. Can you picture it? In a few months, every time I try to sit in or get out of that mushy mess, it'll be like harpooning Moby Dick."

"So you don't mind?"

"Mind? I've been fantasizing about unloading that thing since after the third week I moved in here." Eliza sighed. "We'll go shopping together and pick out something we both can live with… or be blamed for." She laughed. "I mean now that we're official, this will be your jurisdiction."

"Sounds like a plan," Tom said, holding Eliza's head in his hands "But I keep telling you, sweetheart. Anywhere you go is my jurisdiction."

THE END

Eliza's Bonus Recipes

Dangerously Spicy Vegetarian Tortilla Soup
  (submitted by Tara Jepson)

Ingredients:
  4 tablespoons olive oil
  ¼ bag tortilla chips, crushed
  1 medium onion, chopped
  2 cloves of garlic, minced
  1 tablespoon paprika
  2 teaspoons ground cumin
  1 teaspoon ground coriander
  1 teaspoon chili powder
  1/4 teaspoon cayenne pepper (omit for a milder
version, add more for a truly *dangerous* soup)
  1 (28-oz.) can crushed tomatoes, juice and all
  4 cups vegetable broth
  1 to 1 1/2 teaspoons salt, to taste
 cracked black pepper
  1 (14-oz.) can black beans, drained and rinsed
fresh corn sliced from 2 ears of corn or 1 can sweet corn
niblets
  1 small jalapeño, seeds and ribs removed and thinly
sliced

Directions:
  In a large, heavy bottom pot, heat oil over medium-
high heat. Reduce the heat to medium heat and add
onions. Cook until translucent and just browned, about
3 to 5 minutes. Add garlic and cook for 1 minute more.
Add paprika, cumin, coriander, chili powder, and
cayenne pepper. Stir and cook for 1 minute more.
  Add the crushed tomatoes, juice and all. Stir to
combine. Add the vegetable broth, salt, and a good
sprinkling of black pepper. Use blender to blend the

mixture until halfway to smooth. Return back to the pot and heat over low heat.

Add beans, corn, and jalapeño and lightly simmer about 20 minutes.

To serve, spoon into bowls and top with crushed tortilla chips, and adorn with (optional) a sprinkling of cheddar cheese, a few slices of avocado, and sour cream. and/or Tabasco/ hot sauce to taste.

Soup will last, in an airtight container in the refrigerator, for up to 5 days.

Makes 4-6 servings.

Suspiciously Delicious Sloppy Joes
  (submitted by Jessica Sanchez)

Ingredients
    1 Tbsp. Olive Oil
    1/2 cup chopped green bell pepper
    1 cup minced onion (one medium onion)
    1/2 cup finely chopped celery
    2 cloves minced garlic
    ½ teaspoon salt
    1 ¼ lb. lean ground beef
    ½ cup Ketchup
    1 15 oz. can fire roasted diced tomatoes
    1 Tbsp. Worcestershire sauce
    1 Tbsp. red wine vinegar
    2 Tbsp. brown sugar
    Pinch cayenne pepper
    Pinch ground cracked pepper
    4-6 hamburger buns

Directions:

Heat olive oil in a large sauté pan on medium high heat. Add the chopped onion, bell pepper and celery. Cook, stirring occasionally until onions are translucent, about 5 more minutes. Add the minced garlic and cook for 30 more seconds. Remove from heat. Remove vegetables from the pan to a medium sized bowl, set aside. Using the same pan (or you can cook the meat at the same time as the vegetables in a separate pan to save time), crumble the ground beef into the pan. You will likely need to do this in two batches, otherwise you will crowd the pan and the beef won't easily brown. Sprinkle with salt. Do not stir the ground beef, just let it cook until it is well browned on one side. Then flip the pieces over and brown the second side. Use a slotted spoon to remove the ground beef from the pan (can add to the set-aside vegetables) and repeat with the rest of the ground beef. If you are using extra lean beef, you will likely not have any excess fat in the pan. If you are using 16% or higher, you may have excess fat. Strain off all but 1 tablespoon of the fat.

Return the cooked ground beef and vegetables to the pan. Use a wooden spoon to break up any chunks of ground beef into smaller bits. Add the ketchup, diced tomatoes, Worcestershire sauce, vinegar and brown sugar to the pan. Stir to mix well. Add cayenne pepper to taste.

Portion out mixture into hamburger buns.

Makes 4-6 servings.

ABOUT THE AUTHOR

 Amy Beth Arkawy is the author of the Eliza Gordon Mystery series: *Killing Time, Dead Silent,* (Mystery & Mayhem Award winner, American Cozy category) and several plays, including: *Psychic Chicken Soup* (McLaren Comedy Award nominee); *Full Moon, Saturday Night; Rage Amongst Yourselves; Crazy Vivian Doesn't Shop at Bloomie's Anymore, The Lost Mertz* and *The Postman Always Writes Twice.* Her work has been produced in New York City and across the country and featured in several anthologies. Her fiction is featured in *Chasing the Codex*, the Cozy Cat Press group mystery and the short story collections *Fiction Noir* and *Backdrafts.* Her articles and reviews have appeared in myriad publications and web sites including: *The Week*; *Atlantic Wire; The New York Observer*; *The Fairfield County Weekly*; and *News Junkie Post*, where she served as Arts and Culture Editor for three years. Amy Beth has talked her way across the dial as a radio DJ and talk show host. She now hosts the Media Bytes award-winning Internet radio show/podcast *The Amy Beth Arkawy Show*, featuring conversations with notable and emerging voices in the arts and pop culture. She also helps others find their voices through her work as a creativity coach and writing teacher.

Acknowledgments

Writing is a solitary profession, but beyond the muses, several people have guided my often wayward journey. Thanks to family and friends who have offered steadfast support and often early readership including: Susan Arkawy, Shana Brown, Neil Wendt, Daria Conte, Jeff Weiskopf, Charley Betz, Julie Bowen and the I-Man, Isaac Neufield. Gratitude, too, to Elaine Acosta, the pied piper of book clubs and the clever members of the Westchester Sleuth Circle, as well as all the enthusiastic bloggers, podcasters and readers who have embraced these characters and their stories and helped spread the word. I am lucky to have found such a generous community of authors, especially the lively Cozy Cat Press family. Its publisher, Patricia Rockwell, who has grown her mighty independent press into a thriving and award-winning enterprise in a few short years, continues to garner my admiration. Thank you for saving the Eliza Gordon mystery series, not once, but twice. I am forever grateful to the members of the late lamented Schoolhouse Theater's Playwright's Workshop; that eclectic array of theater artists helped me reclaim my creativity when it was on life support. And life-long gratitude to Doris Patrao, Allan Gurganus, Louise Meriwether and George Cuomo, teachers whose lessons of encouragement, craft and discipline are imbued in my soul. I am honored to pay those lessons forward in my work as a creativity coach and writing teacher. I am privileged to share this journey, this quest with my clients and students. Together we continue to unravel the mysteries of creative exploration. And to the memory of my father, Norman Arkawy, I will forever cherish your wisdom and honor your aspirations. Our conversation continues.

www.ingramcontent.com/pod-product-compliance
Lightning Source LLC
Chambersburg PA
CBHW020313260626
47156CB00004B/1203